DAVID O'CONNELL

The SMiDGENS

UNITED

Illustrated by
SEB BURNETT

BLOOMSBURY
CHILDREN'S BOOKS
LONDON OXFORD NEW YORK NEW DELHI SYDNEY

BLOOMSBURY CHILDREN'S BOOKS
Bloomsbury Publishing Plc
50 Bedford Square, London WC1B 3DP, UK
29 Earlsfort Terrace, Dublin 2, Ireland

BLOOMSBURY, BLOOMSBURY CHILDREN'S BOOKS and the
Diana logo are trademarks of Bloomsbury Publishing Plc

First published in Great Britain in 2023 by Bloomsbury Publishing Plc

A catalogue record for this book is available from the British Library

ISBN: PB: 978-1-5266-4060-4;
eBook: 978-1-5266-4058-1; ePDF: 978-1-5266-4059-8

2 4 6 8 10 9 7 5 3 1

Printed and bound in Great Britain by CPI Group (UK) Ltd,
Croydon CR0 4YY

MIX
Paper | Supporting
responsible forestry
FSC® C171272

To find out more about our authors and books visit www.bloomsbury.com
and sign up for our newsletters

To Jodie, Emily and Molly

1

Footprints

Gafferty Sprout leaned heavily against the base of the massive wall of ice and watched her breath eddy into wispy clouds. It had taken all her effort to descend the entirety of the sheer, frosted surface. Above her, Dad was following the path she'd already taken, his dark brown beetle coat standing out against the white ice. She waited nervously as he picked his way from one rough ledge to another, his big strong fingers cautiously searching for handholds.

'There are places Smidgens shouldn't go and this is one of them,' he muttered.

'There's a pin hook just to your left,' she called up to him. 'I left it there for you to hang on to.'

'Thank you kindly, daughter dearest,' Dad said, gritting his teeth and panting noisily as he reached for the little metal peg. 'What a pleasure it is to be honoured with your expert company on this little jaunt of ours.'

Gafferty grinned. The spider costume she wore – Hive Clan Smidgens always dressed as insects or creepy-crawlies – gave her confidence when climbing. She had gone first to test the ice's strength. Dad had grumbled uneasily, but it made sense as she was so much lighter than him. He was beginning to have faith in her judgement, allowing her to take risks. It was a new sensation for him, one she knew he hated almost as much as she relished her new sense of responsibility. She liked being trusted. It made her feel grown-up.

'There. That was *easy*.' He landed next to her with a soft thump, his broad feet flattening the finely powdered snow that lay around them as far as the eye could see. It was a desolate landscape littered with jagged ice slabs, surrounded by high silvery cliffs. A thin mist veiled the horizon. 'Just a short walk now.' Dad pointed to a low mound; its smooth sides shone white. 'Your mum spotted it yesterday on her scavenger trip but didn't have time to stop and investigate properly.'

They warily made their way over the frozen surface, careful to avoid any icy drifts that might hide a crevasse that could easily swallow them up. Gafferty couldn't resist throwing a quick snowball at her father when he wasn't looking.

'Keep your mind on the job, you giddy dream-bucket!' he scolded, brushing the ice from his jacket. Gafferty's face reddened in shame, then felt a sharp blow as a snowball landed on her cheek and exploded. 'And learn to throw,' Dad chuckled. 'Your old man's still a better shot than you, if nothing else.'

Soon they reached the foot of the mound. Dad pulled a metal blade from his coat and sank its point into the hill's surface. The ground split as he dragged the knife through it, a hole opening in the thin covering. Solid green globes, the size of one of Dad's hands, poured out and rolled over the ice at their feet.

'Buried treasure,' Dad said with satisfaction. 'Peas. And as cold as a ghost's kiss.'

Gafferty shivered. She'd had close contact with ghosts before. Not a kiss, mind you, but as near as she'd ever wanted to be. One of the few humans she'd encountered, the villainous Claudia Slymark, had kept ghosts as her servants to do her wicked commands. Gafferty suspected she might meet them again but tried not to think about it too much.

'You wouldn't think it was the middle of the summer, would you?' she said instead. She peered up at the pale light far over their heads. She could almost imagine it as the winter sun and that they were wandering through some barren frozen wasteland, not stood at the bottom of a freezer in the frozen food aisle of McTavish's Supermarket, illuminated by a dull orange lamp hanging from grubby plastic ceiling tiles. Outside the shop the actual sun would just be rising, heralding the start of a long, warm day for both Smidgens and Big Folk alike.

Mum had discovered the Big Folk shopworkers were clearing out their huge freezers to defrost them, and an unnoticed bag of peas buried in the ice was a prime scavenger target. Climbing into the freezer had been tricky, especially for someone only seven centimetres tall, but it had given Gafferty another chance to prove herself to Dad.

She removed her backpack and took out a plastic bag lined with tinfoil. It would keep the peas cool until they could get them back home and into the cooking pot. She swiftly collected the vegetables and had just filled the bag when she saw them: tracks in the ice. No, footprints!

Smidgen-sized prints. They were some distance away, hugging the line of the freezer wall. She silently nudged Dad and pointed. He saw the prints and frowned, glancing quickly about to confirm they were alone as far as it was possible to see.

'Could they be Mum's?' whispered Gafferty.

'She didn't set foot in here. It's too dangerous for one of us by ourselves.'

They jogged over to take a closer look.

'See here!' said Dad, waving at a patch of flattened ice powder. There were broken pieces of solid ice lying around it. 'This is where they came in. It looks like they might have fallen at least part of the way.'

'Do you think there's more than one of them?'

'Possibly. It's difficult to tell, the way the ice has been trampled.'

'It's got to be the Burrow Clan!' said Gafferty. 'They've come back to the Big Folk town already. But why here?'

'There's one of the main Tangle routes nearby. Perhaps they're exploring the Smidgen tunnels and took a detour for food, and one of them has fallen in the freezer by accident.'

Gafferty frowned. She hadn't even known other Smidgens existed until a few months ago. Now she knew there were many of them, but their history was troubled. Of the three clans of Smidgens, the Burrow Clan were the most unfriendly, particularly after their precious Great Jewel was stolen by a Roost Clan Smidgen called Crumpeck before finding its way into Claudia's hands. Gafferty and her friends had been lumbered with the blame! All three clans – the Burrow, the Roost and Gafferty's own clan of the Hive – should have been working together, but Claudia had set them at odds with each other.

'I bet they're here to find and take back the Great Jewel,' she said.

'Whatever they're doing, we know one thing for certain.'

'What's that?'

'There are tracks in, but no tracks out, Gafferty. *They're still here …*'

2

Frozen Fools

'We should find them and talk to them,' she hissed as they ran back to their packs.

'No, we shouldn't.' Dad stuffed a few more peas into his rucksack before hurriedly slinging it over his back. 'There's a time and a place for having a nice chat with a cheese-and-pineapple kebab and a cup of berry juice. Stuck at the bottom of a deep freeze with a rat-riding, Burrow-bothering soldier is not it.'

'But it's a chance for us to make friends,' Gafferty persisted, but Dad was unmoved.

'Come on, Gafferty – let's get out of here. Staying safe is our priority now. What's Rule Two of the Smidgens?'

'*Don't do anything flipping stupid.*'

'Precisely.'

Gafferty knew better than to push Dad when there was a hint of thunder in his voice. They followed their own footprints back the way they had come. They had almost reached the base of the freezer wall when they heard a soft pattering from behind. Gafferty risked a glance. A rat galloped towards them, its breath steaming into clouds, with a fur-clad, bearded Smidgen astride its back. Gafferty grabbed her father's arm in alarm. As the rider neared, she could see his coat was torn and there were scratches on his face – Dad must have been right about the accidental fall into the freezer. The soldier carried a spear and scowled menacingly as his steed bore down on them.

'I guess he's not in the mood to talk after all,' Gafferty said as they both broke into a sprint.

'Told you so,' muttered Dad.

They scrambled up the wall of ice, using the footholds and handholds they had made on their way down. Dad shoved Gafferty up ahead of him, trying to shield her from any possible spear-throwing. Once she was in front, he kicked at the ice so that chunks broke away from it and fell on to the Burrow soldier below. The rat circled the ground beneath the escaping Smidgens, its nose twitching furiously as its rider considered what to do next.

'Can rats climb?' Gafferty asked between breaths.

'Yes. They're good climbers. Whether our friend here can hang on to its back at the same time is another question.'

'He's found the answer to that question already ...'

The rat leaped up the wall, the rider clinging on to its fur tightly, all the time urging it onward with angry cries. Occasionally its paws slipped against the smooth surface as it tried to maintain its grip, but despite this, and the extra weight on its back, the creature made steady progress. Gafferty reached the top of the freezer and turned to see it gaining on them. She hurriedly grabbed Dad's hand and helped him up the last few steps.

They scampered along the edge of the freezer until they could go no further. A gap separated them from a neighbouring shelf that was laden with bottles of ice cream toppings, jars of sugar strands and chocolate buttons. It was only a narrow gap but the enormous drop to the floor below made Gafferty dizzy. There wasn't time to hesitate. They held hands and jumped together, then darted behind the display to catch their breath, listening to the scraping sounds of the rat valiantly clawing its way to the top of the freezer. It wasn't giving up.

'We can't let him follow us home,' said Dad. 'We need a plan. It's time for Rule Four.'

Rule Four: *if in doubt, make it up*. Gafferty scanned the shelf for something that could help them.

'Dad – maple syrup!' She pointed to a row of bottles of brown glossy liquid.

'A sticky solution for a sticky problem,' said Dad. 'Good thinking, Gafferty.'

Working together, they pushed one of the bottles clear of the rest.

'Heave!' At Dad's command they both shoved as hard as they could against the plastic container. It wobbled briefly, then fell on its side with a satisfying thud. 'We have to get the top off it somehow.'

'There's no time!' Gafferty pointed to the freezer. The rat had scrambled out and was tottering uneasily along the icy edge towards them, clearly determined not to make the same mistake twice and tumble into the frozen depths again. Its rider wore a smug smile. He was sure that he would catch his quarry now. There was no way two Smidgens on foot could outrun a rat!

Gafferty grabbed her knife from the bag. She raised the blade over her head, then plunged it into the bottle's side. The plastic split, and syrup oozed slowly from the break.

'That's not going to do much good,' said Dad. 'Hey, what are you doing now, girl?' Gafferty had jumped on to his back and was climbing on to his shoulders.

'Help me up!' she said. 'I'm going to make a bit of a splash!'

Dad stood steady as she balanced on his shoulders. Gafferty waited for the right moment – she had to time this precisely!

'Gafferty,' Dad growled. 'This had better work.'

'It will! Just a second more …'

The rat was almost upon them. They could practically feel the creature's whiskers tickling their faces when –

'Now!' Gafferty yelled as she launched herself into

the air, landing on the damaged bottle with her full weight. Syrup erupted from the split, exploding in the rat's face and bubbling out and over the shelf. The rat squealed in surprise. Dad belly-flopped on to the bottle beside his daughter, sending another surge of syrup over the rider and adding to the sticky brown slick that surrounded the rat. Rider and steed were stuck fast. The rat would have no choice but to lick its fur and paws clean and eat its way out of this very tasty trap. The rider howled with fury, raising his spear to throw at the enemy Smidgens who had outwitted him … but they had already vanished into the shadows.

3

A Sliver of Hope

Gafferty and Dad hurried from the supermarket as fast as they could. They kept a sharp eye out for any more hostile Burrow Smidgens all the way to the chocolate factory that hid their cavern home, the Hive. There was no disguising the worry on their faces when they delivered the bag of chilled peas to the Sprout family kitchen.

'You'll need to tell Lady Strigida at the Roost about this,' Mum said, once they'd described what had happened. She chopped the peas into chunks with a fury that made the kitchen table shake. 'I won't have any trouble on our doorstep again! After a full-scale battle so close to our own home – it's intolerable! These young ones shouldn't have to live through such goings-on.'

Gafferty recalled the fight with the Burrow Smidgens up in the chocolate factory. Although she had managed to befriend a Burrow girl named Quigg, it hadn't been enough to bring peace. Gafferty's baby brother, Grub, babbled his agreement with his mother from a high chair and blew a snot bubble for extra emphasis. Gafferty didn't need any further encouragement.

'I'll go to the Roost now,' she said, cleaning the syrup off her knife in the sink. The glass blade shone in the cosy light from the stove. It was such a small thing, but it was an important one – just like the stolen Great Jewel, the glass knife was a piece of the broken Mirror of Trokanis, an ancient magical treasure that Claudia Slymark was desperate to find.

'You're not wandering off anywhere on your own!' said Dad.

'Gobkin can come with me.' She grabbed the shoulder of her younger brother, who was sitting at the table chiselling flakes off a salt crystal to season the soup. He looked up from his task in surprise.

'I can?' he said. Gafferty was normally reluctant to take him anywhere. She didn't have the patience to babysit her siblings.

'Yes – if we meet a rat I can throw you in front of it.

They like to eat little boy Smidgens, I've heard. It'll give me a chance to escape.'

Gobkin was not amused but grabbed his fly eye goggles anyway. Mum looked unconvinced.

'Are you sure about this, Gaff?' she said. Gafferty slung her scavenger bag back on to her shoulder.

'Small Smidgens can move more swiftly and hide more easily. And we need to act now.'

Mum and Dad glanced at each other uneasily, but Gafferty had proved them wrong before. With a kiss from both of their parents the two young Smidgens headed off.

In spite of their fears of encountering another scout from the Burrow Clan, the Tangle – the maze of Smidgen tunnels that ran underneath the human town – was as deserted as usual, apart from the occasional beetle or worm. When they arrived at the Roost, tucked into the attic of an ancient tower that formed part of the hotel, they found the little Smidgen community was as bustling as ever. The golden light of morning tumbled through the tower's giant window and bathed the hidden town in its warmth. But Gafferty could feel the tension in the air. Many of the Smidgens, in their characteristic bird disguises, were armed. Crumpeck – one of their own – had been responsible for stealing the Great Jewel from the Burrow, and had then been kidnapped by Claudia along with it. The Burrow Clan had attacked the Hive in retaliation, and now no one felt safe.

Lady Strigida was expecting them.

'It's the Burrow Clan you've come to see me about, isn't it?' the old Smidgen said as she led them into her house. 'Our glider scouts have spotted their rat riders. Not many, mind you – there's no sign of any army. These seem to be spies, working alone or in pairs. As soon as they think they've been seen they disappear. They're clearly not keen to talk to us. Too busy looking for their Jewel.'

'Yes – I've just seen one of them!' said Gafferty. She and Gobkin threw themselves down on one of the hotel soap-dish sofas, clearing space amongst the piles of yellowed scrolls and books scattered everywhere. As leader of the Roost Clan, Lady Strigida knew lots about the lore and culture of the Smidgens, a knowledge that had proved invaluable lately. She had remembered the tales about the Mirror of Trokanis and the fact that it had been broken into pieces. Two of the three pieces had been found, but where was the third?

Just then, a familiar face appeared at the doorway.

'Will!' said Gafferty. The boy grinned at her.

'I heard you were here,' he said, joining them on the sofa. 'Have you come for more flying lessons?'

'No chance! At least not with you, after all the times we've crashed. We're here to talk about the Burrow Clan, and what we're going to do about them.'

'And what we're going to do about Crumpeck, don't forget.'

'That strange old fossil? His obsession with the Mirror caused a lot of this trouble.'

'We can't abandon him, even though he's disgraced himself,' said Strigida. 'We've been searching for him ever since he was taken. Claudia Slymark was staying in the hotel, so obviously her room was the first place we looked.'

'Did you find him?'

'No!' Will said before Strigida could reply. 'But we couldn't find Claudia either. She's vanished!'

'What do you mean?'

'She didn't check out of the hotel. All her stuff was there but she wasn't. After a few days, the hotel removed everything because she hadn't paid her bill.'

'Maybe she had to leave in a hurry?' suggested Gafferty hopefully.

'It doesn't sound like Claudia,' observed Gobkin quietly. He'd been kidnapped by the thief once. 'She's cunning and not the forgetful or hasty type. It sounds odd to me.'

'Everything's odd!' sighed Gafferty. 'Nothing is as it should be! We should be friends with the Burrow, not enemies.'

'That's why we've been looking for Crumpeck,' said Strigida. 'If we can find him, or Claudia, we might be able to find the Jewel. And if we can get the Jewel back to the Burrow, we might be able to convince them that we mean well.'

'But if Claudia is gone,' said Gafferty, 'how are we going to do that?'

Lady Strigida smiled.

'There's still hope,' she said. 'Thanks to your friend Noah.'

Noah was a human boy, one of the few Big Folk to know about the existence of the Smidgens. He'd helped Gafferty and Will when they were at the Burrow and was familiar with Claudia and her ghosts. He and Will had even worked out a way to send messages to each other: when he had something important to tell the Smidgens, Noah would leave a picture of a bird on his bedroom window sill where the Roost glider scouts could see it.

'Noah's mum works as a cleaner and does shifts at the

hotel,' explained Lady Strigida. 'And she found out what happened to the luggage after Claudia disappeared. The hotel had an address for her, in a Big Folk town called London, and her suitcases have been sent to the local post office to be forwarded onwards. Noah's mum overheard the hotel manager having an argument with someone on a *tellyfone*.'

'A what?' said Gafferty.

'It's a box the Big Folk use to shout at one another while avoiding having to be in the same room with them,' said Gobkin. 'It's in *The Big Book of Big Folk Facts*.'

'The disagreement was over who would pay for the delivery of the suitcases to London,' continued Strigida. 'They couldn't decide and so the luggage is still sitting in the sorting office.'

'We have to go and look,' said Gafferty. 'There may be clues in Claudia's belongings about Crumpeck and the Great Jewel! It's our only chance to get the Jewel back, otherwise the Burrow might never trust us again.'

She looked at Will and grinned. It was the perfect task for two small Smidgens.

4

A Dangerous Bargain

Claudia Slymark was decidedly unhappy at the change in her circumstances. She couldn't bring herself to think that she was actually *dead*, as *dead* had such a final sound to it. She preferred to think of herself as *transformed*, which suggested there was a possibility, even if it was a remote one, that the alteration was reversible. Either way, she was a ghost. And what was more, a prisoner, stuck inside a small glass bottle at the cruel whim of a particularly creepy sort of sorcerer.

She had finally got hold of a piece of the Mirror of Trokanis for her mysterious client when she had discovered that he had been in league with the revolting Osiris Ribbons, the undertaker or necromancer or whatever he called himself, who claimed ownership of the bottled ghosts, tools that had been so useful to Claudia for so long. He even said he had created them. So with her client's help, he had taken them back and, what was more, added her to the collection. If nothing else, it was a breach of contract. Claudia was a professional and expected the same from her clients. She might be a ghost and she might be trapped but she was *furious*. This business was not over yet.

In the meantime, she'd had no choice but to play along. The other ghosts, Totherbligh and Hinchsniff, had been unexpectedly sympathetic, as Mr Ribbons was no friend of theirs. He kept the bottles on a shelf in the dark basement of the funeral parlour. They were surrounded by coffins, some of which were occupied. At least with Claudia, the ghosts had got to travel and see the world.

'Don't worry, Miss Slymark,' said Totherbligh, peering at her through the glass from his bottle. 'He's done without us for this long, perhaps he'll leave us alone.'

'If we're lucky,' grumbled Hinchsniff from her other side. 'What if he wants the bottles for something else? They're magic crystal. It's useful. What if he wants to –' his voice dropped to a whisper – '*evict* us?'

'Then you'd … *we'd* be free, wouldn't we?' said

Claudia, turning towards him. It had taken her a while to get used to controlling her ghostly form. 'Isn't that a good thing?'

'He'd have to destroy us,' Hinchsniff whimpered. 'We're tied to the bottle. He'd drag us out and stretch us and stretch us until the magic link snapped and we'd dissipate. Fade away into nothing, our souls lost forever.'

There had to be another way. Claudia didn't know much about magic, but there was always another way. A spell could always be undone. One thing at a time. First, she wanted to get revenge on the person who had got her into this mess – the mysterious client who'd sent her on the hunt for the Mirror. But how?

At that moment they heard the heavy steps of Mr Ribbons descending into the basement. He moved without hurry; he'd lived so long he never needed to rush. His black eyes, two small currants in the smooth white pudding of his head, darted around the shadows of the room like a lizard's. He approached the shelf, his dark tongue flicking around his teeth. He looked hungry. Claudia heard the other bottles trembling.

'My little friends,' Mr Ribbons said with a sinister chuckle. 'So good to have you home again after all this time. I hope you're settling in, Miss Slymark.'

Claudia wasn't going to be intimidated.

'Cramped inside stolen property? We could have done a deal, Ribbons.'

Mr Ribbons's eyes flashed annoyance for a second but then he grinned.

'I have no need for deals. The bottles are mine. I made them. Magic crystal is also valuable in its own right. I may have other uses for your home if you are not careful.'

'You could have taken the crystal I had with me. The piece of glass I retrieved from the Smidgens. Why didn't you?'

The man sniffed.

'It was hardly worth my while. A broken trinket. Its value was limited.'

'By itself, perhaps. But the pieces together would have created something priceless.'

Mr Ribbons raised an eyebrow. There was a brief look of confusion on his face. Brief, but Claudia saw it.

'You weren't told what it did, were you?' she said. 'The Mirror of Trokanis. You don't know what it could do if it's put back together. I'm not surprised. It's so powerful, I would want to keep it secret too. What I could do with that kind of power ...'

It worked. Ribbons was interested.

'You must tell me more, Miss Slymark,' he said. He spoke in the same polite tone, but it wasn't a request. It was an order. Claudia kept her nerve.

'Better than that,' she said, 'I can help you get hold of it. I'm a thief after all. It's what I do best. You can ask these other two.'

'Oh yes, master,' said Totherbligh. 'She is famous for her skill.'

'The finest in the business, master,' added Hinchsniff with a weak smile.

'I said I have no need for deals,' growled Mr Ribbons. His eyes burned angrily. 'And you are certainly not in a position to make bargains, Slymark!'

'I know,' Claudia said, keeping her cool. 'I'm not trying to make a bargain. The only one who can possibly benefit is you. I'm offering to help you. I'm offering my talents. But to put my talents to their best use, I need information. All the information you have about my former client. Who he is, and how you met, for instance.'

Ribbons's anger subsided. He seemed to consider the matter.

'Very well,' he said finally. 'I'll tell you. I suppose it can do no harm now. Your client knew the bottles were mine, but that is no secret to those who make magic their business. He contacted me via a letter. He told me he knew where I could find you. I'll admit it had been very difficult to keep track of you – another one of your talents, I assume. So I accepted his proposal. Luckily for me, you turned up at the post office at the same time I did. There you have it.'

'And my client? His name?'

'Trokanis,' said Mr Ribbons. 'His name is Trokanis.'

5

Return to the Smidgenmoot

With the help of a couple of matchstick torches, Gafferty and Will picked their way through the rubble of the collapsed tunnel. Gafferty glanced at her atlas of the Tangle every now and again, checking the progress of their journey. They'd had to detour around several other damaged passageways and a flooded cave already.

'I can't believe Lady Strigida is letting us do this,' said Will, his voice trembling slightly. Gafferty smiled. When she'd first met Will, he'd been nervous and a bit of a worrier, but he'd grown much bolder thanks to the scrapes Gafferty had dragged him into. If his voice shook it was more likely he was excited about the adventure ahead than scared. In turn, his good nature had taught her to think more of others, to understand what it was like to be a part of a community and to be less head-strong – although she'd never admit it.

'Strigida knows I can find my way around the Tangle,' Gafferty said. 'And she knows you'll keep an eye on me. Besides, this shouldn't be dangerous, as long as we don't meet any of the Burrow Clan.'

'I hope Quigg didn't get into too much trouble with her chief. She was an odd one, but I think she liked you in her way.'

'I liked her.' Gafferty sighed. 'Why does the world make it so hard to be friends? People go looking for things to disagree on. It's so silly.'

'You're quite good at disagreeing too, you know. You and Wyn have bumped heads a few times.'

Gafferty laughed. Will's brother was an even match for her when it came to an argument, but he wasn't all bad. He had offered to give Gobkin a ride back to the Hive in his glider, which Gob had taken up enthusiastically. Meanwhile, she and Will had been sent on an expedition.

'I hope Claudia Slymark hasn't taken Crumpeck to this London place,' said Will as they scrambled over a rockfall. 'No Smidgen has ever left the town before, as far as I know. We've no idea how far away anywhere in the Big Folk world is.'

'Let's not get ahead of ourselves,' Gafferty said, studying the atlas once more. 'We've got to get to the sorting office first. This bit of the Tangle hasn't been used for a very long time. I'm beginning to think we should have taken your wings and flown there after all.'

'It's too dangerous. You heard what Wyn said. There's a colony of crows living on the roof.' He shivered. 'They'd have us for breakfast.'

'Don't talk about breakfast or I'll get hungry. It's almost lunchtime and we've hardly got anywhere.' Gafferty shone her torch down the tunnel. 'And I don't think we're going to get further here either.'

The light fell on a wall of broken stone. Their path was completely blocked.

'Another dead end!' groaned Will. 'Now what?'

Gafferty consulted the atlas.

'There's still a way. We'll have to backtrack for a bit and then go via the Smidgenmoot. There's a passage from there that goes directly to the post office.'

Will's face fell.

'Do we have to go there?' he said.

They'd been through the Smidgenmoot together once

before. The Roost Clan regarded it as forbidden and haunted, and kept clear of it. But Gafferty thought the enormous cave was a thing of wonder, with its row upon row of seats encircling a huge central stage of black stone. It felt like somewhere that had seen history happen. Hundreds of years ago it had acted as a meeting place for all three Smidgen clans, where they shared news and made decisions together. For Gafferty, the Smidgenmoot was a reminder of a time when the clans were united and showed what they could achieve when they worked as one.

'We'll just go across it,' she said, pointing out the route in the atlas. 'We won't be there long.'

Secretly she was glad of the chance to revisit the Smidgenmoot. She knew somehow it was linked to the Mirror. The last time they had been through the cave her glass knife had behaved oddly, glowing with a shimmering light that changed colour, as strange voices spoke to her inside her mind. A similar thing had happened at the Burrow, when she had encountered the Great Jewel. The Smidgenmoot was part of the mystery of the Mirror and Gafferty wanted to know more.

She led the way back and through the tunnels, thankfully finding no new obstacles to block their path.

Eventually they arrived at the Smidgenmoot. It was just as Gafferty remembered it, majestic and awe-inspiring, their whispers echoing from its curved stone walls like the sound of gentle waves on a shore. The passageway had come out into the middle of one of the seating tiers. They scampered down to the central platform.

'The way to the sorting office is down a tunnel that leads from here,' Gafferty said.

'Your knife's glowing again,' said Will. 'Just like last time.'

Pink light was pouring out of Gafferty's bag. She took out the knife, which, sure enough, was lit up almost as bright as their torches. Tiny glowing spots emerged from the blade and flew around their heads. Gafferty heard fragments of voices in her mind, just as she had before.

'As we get closer to the centre it gets brighter,' she said. 'I wonder if this is where the Mirror comes from. I wonder if this is its home.'

A figure rose up from one of the seats near the platform, casting a gaunt, twitching shadow across the chamber in the flickering light.

'Yes, this is its home,' it said. 'And this is where it will return.'

6

An Unexpected Reunion

'Crumpeck?' Gafferty could barely get the word out. Was it really him?

It was. The figure was staring at the knife in the same greedy way he had when they had first met. He didn't even seem to notice the two Smidgens were there.

'We thought we wouldn't ever see you again!' said Will, running up to the old man.

Crumpeck came out of his daze and seemed to see Will for the first time.

'Willoughby, my lad,' he said, smiling weakly and patting him on the shoulder. 'Fancy seeing you here.'

'We're here because of you!' said Will. 'We've been trying to find you, Crumpeck. What happened to you?'

The old Smidgen looked confused for a moment.

'What happened? Oh, you mean that dreadful Big Folk woman with the grabbing hands. Claudia Thingamabob. It was quite a surprise when she turned up, wasn't it? I was manhandled in a most inconsiderate manner. Completely outrageous!'

'How did you get away from her?' asked Gafferty. 'You've been missing for days. And how did you end up here of all places? What happened to the Great Jewel?'

Crumpeck frowned at all the questions.

'I don't really know,' he said faintly. 'It's all a bit hazy.'

It was Will's turn to frown.

'I think he might be in shock,' he whispered to Gafferty. 'Perhaps it's affected his memory. We should get him home.'

Gafferty chewed her lip. It was typical of Will to think kindly of Crumpeck. She, on the other hand, couldn't help feeling suspicious about his unexplained reappearance. Claudia wouldn't have just let him go. She would have found a use for him like she did with Gobkin. He'd been the bait in a trap. Could this be another trap of Claudia's?

'What was that you said a minute ago?' she asked. 'The Smidgenmoot being the home of the Mirror?'

Crumpeck's eyes brightened.

'This is where the Mirror stood, the histories say. In an arch of stone.' He walked over to the platform. At one end was a pile of rubble that Gafferty had noticed on her first visit to the Smidgenmoot months ago. She had thought it was a broken statue. The older Smidgen stooped and ran his fingers gently over the debris, picking up one of the stones. 'The arch held the Mirror in place like a door. You stepped through it, into the magical portal, a portal that could take you wherever you wished. Can you imagine it?' He sighed as if he could see the doorway opening in front of him. Then his expression changed, his face darkened. 'And this is where the Mirror was shattered. A priceless artefact destroyed! Such a terrible crime. The golden age of the Smidgens was destroyed with it, never to be recovered.' He dashed the stone back to the ground in frustration.

'That's all in the past,' said Gafferty. 'And now we've a chance to make a new future for ourselves.'

'We can never escape the past. It is the past that makes us who we are. Do you remember in the Burrow, the Chief saying that your ancestors were present at the breaking of the Mirror?'

'What?' said Will. 'Gafferty, what is he talking about?'

She nodded. They'd thought Crumpeck had been unconscious at the time, knocked over by an explosion of energy from the Great Jewel. He'd obviously been listening in on her conversation with the Chief, the old sneak!

'It's true,' she said. 'Chief Talpa and I can hear voices coming from the Mirror fragments. I reckon Crumpeck does too. Words, sounds, it doesn't make much sense. Talpa thinks our great-great-whatever-grandparents were there when the Mirror was smashed. That's why we're connected to it in some way.'

'Perhaps they were the ones who destroyed it!' said Crumpeck, his eyes widening suddenly. He grabbed Gafferty by her shoulders. 'We're haunted by the actions of our ancestors. We must make amends!'

Gafferty pulled away from him in alarm.

'Don't be daft! It's not our fault it happened, even if that is true.'

'We need to get you home, Crumpeck,' Will said gently. 'You've had a shock. You're not your normal self. Lady Strigida will know what to do.'

'Botheration to being normal!' snapped Crumpeck. 'Strigida doesn't share my vison. *Normal* people don't. But ...' He paused, as if an idea had just occurred to him.

'But I would like to go home. Yes, there's something there I have to do. Something I have to find.' He started walking back the way they had come. 'Come along, Willoughby!' he called, breaking into a march. 'I haven't got all day!'

Gafferty and Will looked at each other in bewilderment.

'He was eccentric before all this business,' said Will. 'Now he's really gone loopy!'

He hurried after Crumpeck, clambering up the steps into the darkness, but Gafferty didn't move.

'Get him home safely, Will,' she called. 'I'm going to carry on to the sorting office. Just in case there's anything useful there.'

Will waved at her before disappearing into the tunnel. She turned and headed towards the passage that led to the Big Folk post office, her mind full of uneasy thoughts. How had Crumpeck ended up in the Smidgenmoot? Perhaps he had been with Claudia's luggage, stuffed into a bag like a pair of socks, and had wandered here after freeing himself. So why didn't he remember doing it? It was very strange. It was almost as if he had been deliberately left there so that they would find him. But by who? Gafferty's head hurt from all the many questions buzzing through it. So much so that she didn't notice that she was being followed.

7

Mixed Messages

It had been easy for Claudia to find out where Noah went to school. He had told her himself that his mother worked as a cleaner at the golf course. A little ghostly snooping in their records had uncovered the family's address. The nearest school was just a short drive away.

At the lunchtime break, Claudia and Hinchsniff discreetly slid over the school wall and hid themselves behind the sports hall while Mr Ribbons and Totherbligh waited in the not-so-discreet hearse nearby.

'You know what to do,' said Claudia. 'Don't mess it up.'

'You're not my boss any more,' said Hinchsniff resentfully.

'Don't mess it up,' Claudia repeated. She might be a ghost, but her voice had lost none of its commanding tone. Hinchsniff looked at his spectral feet uncomfortably.

'Yes, Miss Slymark.'

'I can see the boy playing football. You approach him while I stay here. He mustn't see me, or the plan won't work.'

Hinchsniff nodded and sailed around the side of the building. Claudia peeped around the corner and watched as he hissed at the boy who was standing nearby. Noah's face fell when he saw the ghost. In the afternoon light it was almost invisible, but Noah was familiar with Hinchsniff's ferret-like features.

'Hey, kid,' Hinchsniff said. 'Come over here. Don't try anything funny.'

'No,' said Noah. 'I don't want anything to do with you. Go away.'

'Now that's just rude. And I thought you were such a nice boy, helping those little people and everything. Well, I want to help too and I've some really important information I know your tiny friends are after. You wouldn't want them to find out you'd kept some important information from them, would you?'

Noah cautiously approached.

41

'What are you doing here, spook?' he asked. 'What are you up to? And where's Claudia? I know she's disappeared.'

'Yes, she's … retired. We're under new management. We're the good guys now.'

'I don't believe you.'

'It's true. We only want to help the rat people … the Smidgens, I mean.'

'Really. And how are you going to do that?'

Claudia watched as Hinchsniff gave him a conspiratorial look. He wasn't a bad actor.

'They're after these bits of glass, right?'

'Maybe.'

'We both know they are. Sounds like a load of nonsense, if you ask me, but each to their own. Anyway, now that we don't work for Claudia, we'd like to assist those sweet little Smidgens, bless 'em. We've got information to help them find those bits of glass.'

Noah rolled his eyes.

'You must think I'm daft,' he said. 'There's no way you'd want to help anybody.'

Hinchsniff attempted to look offended.

'That's hurtful, that is. We only ever did what we were told to do. We want to get on in life. Or, in our case, the afterlife. Just like everyone else.'

'You're not like everyone else,' said Noah. 'Not in any way.'

'Whatever. So here it is: we're no fans of those bits of glass. They're dangerous to ghosts. You can ask Gafferty if you don't believe me. We want to see them out of the way, and I reckon letting the Smidgens have them for safekeeping is the best solution. That way everybody wins.'

Claudia watched Noah's face as he considered this. The boy was no fool.

'All right,' said Noah. 'I still don't believe you but let's talk.'

'Good boy. Now the thing is, we don't know how to get in contact with Gafferty and the others, to share with them this important information that we have.'

'Then tell me and I'll tell them.'

'Oh, no – we couldn't do that. No offence, but we've no reason to trust you any more than you can trust us. We want to tell them in person. Face to tiny little face.'

'Fine. I can send them a message later when I get home from school.'

'Good lad. That wasn't too hard, was it? We can meet here tomorrow, and you can tell me their reply. Deal?'

'Deal.'

The bell rang, summoning Noah back to class. Hinchsniff watched as the boy ran inside the school building, before slinking behind the sports hall.

'It worked,' Hinchsniff said, pleased with himself.

Claudia nodded. Everything was going to plan.

Gafferty had reached the end of the tunnel. Daylight leaked through a floor-to-ceiling gap in the wall in front of her. Stubbing her torch out in the dirt, she pushed her fingers through the gap, and found that with a bit of effort she was able to gently pull the wall to one side.

Machinery noise flooded into the tunnel from the world beyond. The doorway she had made was in the skirting board on one side of an enormous room. It was a place of busyness and bustle, a place of work. Big Folk scurried about in all directions. Some were emptying large grey sacks of letters of all shapes and sizes on to a conveyor belt at the far end of the building. The belt carried the letters into a machine that stacked them into neat bundles which were then picked up by other Big Folk. They took the bundles to a table where the letters were sorted into different shelves that ran the whole length of the wall. Gafferty didn't quite understand what was going on, but Big Folk had odd habits that weren't worth the trouble of thinking about too hard. There was plenty to look at, but what Gafferty couldn't see was Claudia's luggage.

She glanced between the ankles of the passing humans and spotted a door with a sign on it saying *Storeroom*. That sounded promising. She easily slipped unnoticed across the office and scrambled under the door. The room on the other side was filled with towers of boxes and broken machines. Piles of mail – undeliverable for whatever reason – now lay abandoned and forgotten. Gafferty felt an uncomfortable chill. The desolate, cobwebbed room had a sadness and silence to it that made her feel uneasy.

But then she noticed the suitcase. It was one of those ones with hard sides and wheels built into it, a smart, expensive piece of luggage that looked very new and out of place in this graveyard of a storeroom.

'That must be Claudia's!' she said out loud.

There was a sticker stuck to the side with the thief's name printed on it and what Gafferty guessed must be her address. Gobkin was right: it was very odd that the suitcase had been left behind. Where had Claudia gone?

The suitcase was locked with a padlock that had a combination dial. Gafferty was never going to guess the combination – but if the Great Jewel was in there, she had to get it! She took the knife out of her bag and tried to insert the glass blade between the metal teeth of the suitcase's zip. It just fit. As she began to prise the zip apart, she noticed the knife still glowed faintly. It must be a sign the Great Jewel was nearby! But instead of the usual pink light, the knife glowed a dark purple. What did that mean?

The uneasy feeling grew stronger, and she imagined eyes watching her, staring at her back. She turned around suddenly. Right behind her, almost touching, stood a creature unlike anything she had seen before. The creature was like her, a Smidgen, but there was something wild and unearthly about him. He was male and looked old, very old, his skin stretched over his skull until it was almost transparent, his teeth more like fangs. He was dressed in rags, under which Gafferty could see thin, wiry limbs and hands that ended in bony fingers which reached out towards her. Strands of hair fell over his eyes. He gazed at the knife with a fiery intensity. What was a Smidgen doing here? How could such a thing have crept up on her without a sound? She recoiled, her back pressed up against the suitcase.

'Who are you?' she said, her voice trembling.

His eyes flicked from the knife to her face.

'Have no fear. Why should I harm you? We are both the same kind, child. And you have been so good as to return my property to me.' His eyes returned to the knife.

'Your property?'

'Of course. A piece of the Mirror. The Mirror of Trokanis.'

'It belongs to you? I-I don't understand …'

'Can't you guess? Silly child. It belongs to me because I created it. I am Trokanis.'

8

A Face from the Past

'That can't be true!' said Gafferty. 'It's impossible. The Mirror was created hundreds of years ago. Trokanis can't still be alive. He'd be ...' She was about to say 'ancient' when she realised that the Smidgen in front of her looked exactly that.

'Why shouldn't I have lived this long?' Trokanis sighed. 'If I had the power to create such a thing as the Mirror, then extending my lifespan a few centuries would be an easy feat. Perhaps it was a mistake to outlive all those around me – friends, loved ones – but it's too late to undo it.'

He sniffed and rubbed his nose. Gafferty still didn't believe him.

'If you're Trokanis,' said Gafferty, 'tell me why the Mirror was broken.'

His face darkened.

'Fear. Ignorance. My magic-craft could have transformed Smidgen society. The Mirror allowed us to stop fearing the Big Folk, forever scurrying around under their feet, forever hiding. We travelled wherever we needed to go in an instant: food supplies could be reached in seconds. In time, we could have ventured beyond the confines of the town and out into the Big Folk world. But the clans disapproved. They said it was unnatural, it would make us lazy. They were suspicious of magic, and envious of my power.'

'So why didn't you make another?'

'I put so much of my magic into the Mirror that when it was destroyed, I was left with almost nothing. I might have put the pieces back together, but they were separated and taken away, kept where I could not reach them. I was an exile, cast out by the clans.

'But then they argued amongst themselves and became isolated from each other, and Smidgen society began to fail. It broke my heart to see so much greatness lost forever. Until you appeared, I thought I'd never see the pieces of my mirror again. It was my life's work.'

He glanced at the knife that rested in Gafferty's hand.

'See how it glows with a purple light when near me? It knows its maker.'

'You were in the Smidgenmoot that time before when the knife went purple. I knew I'd seen someone!'

'Sometimes I go there to remember. My memory is not so good, and I find the old places help to recall the past. I watched you enter the Smidgenmoot and hid. I'd not encountered another Smidgen in years. I wasn't even sure they still existed. Imagine my surprise to see you with a piece of the Mirror itself! My heart leaped.'

'But why are you living *here*?' Gafferty said a little more gently. 'It's not very … cosy.'

'I can learn things here. I can keep in touch with the doings of the Big Folk world. They send their letters to each other. Filled with information, facts, news, gossip and secrets. It's easy enough to recognise the important messages, to open them and find things out. And send my own letters if necessary.'

He turned and shuffled away, heading towards an old postbox that lay on its side on the floor. It was the kind of postbox that would have been fixed to a wall or street light. Here it was just another piece of abandoned junk. He beckoned her to follow. Gafferty hesitated. This strange old Smidgen might be telling the truth, or he might just be some crazed, lost recluse, but either way he knew something about the Mirror and that information was valuable when the Smidgen histories were so fragmented.

'Letters?' she said, catching up with him. 'Letters to who? Why would you send letters to Big Folk?'

'To get them to do my bidding. To do the things I cannot do. Although I've had the power to keep myself alive this long, I am still frail and old. Humans have made themselves useful to me.' He chuckled. 'Although they didn't always know it.'

He led her through the slot of the postbox, which acted as a door into what Gafferty realised was the old Smidgen's home. It was small and barely furnished. There was only a bed, a chair, a stub of a candle and a box containing a human-sized ink pen nib amongst other odds and ends, which Gafferty guessed he must use to write all his letters. There were no windows of any kind, so the far end of the postbox was hidden in shadow. The old man sat down heavily on the bed.

'What is your name, child? I'd like to know who was clever enough to find a piece of my Mirror.'

'I'm Gafferty Sprout of the Hive.'

'Sprout? Hmmm ... the Sprouts were the leaders of the Hive Clan in my time. Your ancestor Relanna Sprout was there at the breaking, along with the leaders of the two other clans. They each took a piece of the Mirror with them.'

'I saw a painting of this on a wall in the Burrow. A picture with a spider, a bird and a mouse carrying away the pieces of the Mirror. The spider must have been Relanna. You knew my ancestor?'

'Yes.' Trokanis's face was expressionless, but his eyes burned. 'You are much like her. And here you are with that same piece of the Mirror. Destiny is at work, Gafferty Sprout. It brought you here to me. Give me your knife.'

Gafferty looked at the blade in her hand. Voices whispered in her head, the voices from the glass. They sounded urgent, as if trying to make her understand them, trying to warn her of something. Trokanis rose to his feet.

'I want my Mirror back,' he said, more firmly than before. 'Your knife will join the other pieces and the Mirror will be remade. Give it to me.'

Other pieces? What does that mean? Does he know where the Great Jewel is? Gafferty took a step backwards.

She didn't know what to do. If this really was Trokanis then the Mirror belonged to him. He had made it at great cost to himself. She had found the knife by accident. She had no right to it. It would be the simplest thing to give the knife up, to hand it over to this elderly, harmless Smidgen who could find a proper use for it beyond slicing through breadcrumbs or cutting string. She found her hand had moved without her realising, offering him the knife. How did that happen? Something was wrong. These thoughts she was having, they weren't her own – was he controlling her mind? The voices from the knife cried out in fear. They didn't want him to have the knife. It wasn't what she wanted either. She pulled her hand back sharply.

Trokanis's eyes flashed with anger, and he suddenly lunged for her wrist. He was surprisingly strong and gripped her arm tightly as she tried to wriggle free.

'Let go of me!' she yelled, holding on to the knife as best as she could as the old Smidgen attempted to shake it loose.

'Give it back,' Trokanis hissed. 'It is mine!'

Gafferty wrenched herself away from him, the sudden jolt sending her crashing to the floor. Trokanis loomed over her, his hands reaching for her, fingers claw-like.

'I won't let you have it!' Gafferty said, trying to scramble to her feet. 'I don't think you're telling the truth about why the Mirror was broken *or* why you want to remake it. Our ancestors wouldn't have united to stop you without good reason. You may already have the Great Jewel but there's not much you can do with just one piece of the Mirror.'

Trokanis laughed nastily.

'Oh, I've much more than that,' he said. 'As you will soon find out ...'

9

the Power of the Mirror

Trokanis disappeared into the shadows at the rear of the postbox. There was a bright flash of purple light that almost blinded Gafferty and her head filled with the voices once more, the urgent cries desperate and pleading yet at the same time warning her to keep her distance.

The spindly silhouette of Trokanis stood by a large piece of crystal – Gafferty knew instantly that it was the Great Jewel – but that wasn't all. An even bigger crystal lay next to it, and Gafferty could see it neatly slotted into the shape of the Burrow's sacred relic, their jagged edges meeting to form half of a circle.

'It's *another* piece of the Mirror!' she said, her voice

almost a whisper. 'It must be the piece the Roost Clan took.'

Trokanis cackled.

'No! The Roost still have a piece – the last piece. Right under their noses. Soon that will also be mine.'

'But the Mirror was broken into three,' said Gafferty. 'A piece for each clan.'

'That is what they thought. They didn't know I was able to keep a piece for myself. There were four sections of the Mirror and I have always had one. That is what has kept me alive for so long – I've been sustained by the life force within the crystal. But it's been used up over the years. The last of it is gone. Now that I have another piece, I can start to recharge myself, regain my strength.'

He touched the Great Jewel, which pulsed with spots of light. Purple lightning flickered from inside the glass and poured out through the fingers of Trokanis, illuminating the bones under his papery skin. His face became smoother and fuller and his body firmer, younger. Trokanis released the Jewel and sighed, as if he had just finished a satisfying meal.

'You're feeding off it!' Gafferty gasped with horror. 'Eating life force!'

He glared at her and strode towards her, moving swiftly, no longer frail and elderly.

'Now I have new strength, taking that knife from you should be effortless,' he said, his voice clearer than before. 'Then I will have all the pieces of the Mirror bar one.'

Gafferty didn't wait to hear any more. This was wrong, very wrong. She had to get out of there. She needed help. She had blundered into something serious and found herself completely out of her depth, and Rule Four wasn't going to help her now. It was back to the tried and tested Rule Three: *be ready to run, and run fast*.

She turned and fled, running across the room and throwing herself under the door. Which way should she go? Back the way she came – no, too obvious, he would follow. But the other ways were more dangerous. She ran under a rail hung with empty letter sacks, like a set of gigantic grey curtains. Maybe she could hide here and double back when it was safe. Then she heard a violent swishing sound from the end of the rack: something was pushing its way through the bags, pulling them aside and rapidly coming towards her.

Swish. Swish. Swish.

Trokanis was searching for her. She backed up against the wall. Her hand gripped her knife, ready to defend

59

herself. No – he wanted the knife – she should hide it! Panic began to get the better of her. She shrank to the floor, her mind frozen with indecision as the last letter bag was hauled clear. Trokanis paused, a look of triumph on his newly rejuvenated face.

'You cannot escape destiny, Gafferty.' He calmly walked towards her, fingers outstretched. 'Your mind is strong and resists my control, but you will give me the knife. I will not let you stop me remaking the Mirror. And I will not give you another chance.'

She could never outrun him. She stood and was about to offer him the knife when a huge shape barrelled through the mail sacks, knocking Trokanis to the ground. A rat! And it had a rider.

'Found yourself in another mess, have you?'

Gafferty instantly recognised the mouse ears, the furry coat and the crooked stick.

'Quigg! It's you!'

'Of course it is, spider-girl. I suppose you'll be needing me to rescue you.'

She grabbed Gafferty's hand and pulled her up behind her on to the saddle.

'I'm so glad to see you!' Gafferty said, throwing her arms around the girl.

'All right, calm down!' said Quigg, squirming uncomfortably. 'What about Mr Scary McScaryface over there?'

Trokanis looked stunned but was trying to get to his feet.

'Leave him. We need to get out of here now. I'll explain – just go!'

'Gee up, Norbert!' said Quigg.

Gafferty had never ridden a rat before. Norbert could certainly gallop when he put his mind to it. She had to hold on tight to Quigg as the rat darted from one shadowy hiding place to another on his way out of the sorting office. Norbert was well practised at evading humans and quickly found his way to the building's exit, urged onwards by Quigg. Gafferty risked a look back. So far Trokanis was nowhere to be seen.

'How did you find me?' Gafferty asked as she bounced around on the rat's back. Quigg seemed to be able to grip Norbert's sides with her legs, but Gafferty was struggling to keep herself steady. Was there such a thing as rat-sickness?

'Chief Talpa has sent scouts out to search the town for Claudia and the Great Jewel,' said Quigg. 'I was sent out too, to make up for taking your side. I had to prove I was still loyal to the Burrow. I tried to persuade him that you weren't the enemy, Gafferty, I really did, but he just wouldn't listen. I think he felt he'd let the Burrow Clan down when they needed him, and he had to show he was being tough.'

'I'm sorry. But I'm glad you tried. I always knew you would.'

'The Chief made me promise not to go near the chocolate factory in case I warned you about the scouts, so I've been exploring the Tangle with Norbert. We saw you in that great big chamber with Wotsisname and Crumpet. I should have said something then, but ... well, I wasn't sure what you'd say, so I decided to keep quiet and follow you. You always take the more ... interesting route.'

Gafferty managed a laugh. 'Interesting is one way of putting it. Thank goodness you did follow! You turned up in the Smidge of time.'

'What happened? You looked like a mouse that's wandered into a cat show.'

'I found Trokanis. That was him, Mr McScaryface!'

'What?'

'I know it's hard to believe, but the Smidgen who made the Mirror – who made the Great Jewel – is still alive!'

'That's not possible. He can't be!'

'He is!' said Gafferty, almost shouting. 'He's been magically keeping himself alive for centuries and wants to remake the Mirror he created. He wanted to add my knife to his collection of Mirror pieces.'

'He had other bits of the Mirror?'

'Yes! He's already got the Great Jewel and—'

Quigg suddenly pulled hard on the reins and Norbert came to a halt, almost throwing Gafferty off. The Burrow girl turned the rat around.

'What are you doing?' said Gafferty. 'We need to get away from here and warn the Roost.'

'No,' said Quigg. 'We're going back.'

Gafferty was horrified.

'You can't go back. Honestly, Quigg, you don't know what you're up against!'

'If I have a chance to put things right with my clan then I will!' Quigg's face hardened. 'I came here for the Great Jewel. And I'm going to get it.'

10

Feathers and Fury

'No!' yelled Gafferty.

They had stopped in an alley that ran down the side of the building. It was long and narrow, just wide enough for a single human to walk along comfortably. On either side were high walls so that only a little light reached the path even though it was the middle of the day. The rat sniffed the air suspiciously as Gafferty's voice echoed around the alley, his whiskers quivering.

'If I get the Great Jewel back it will fix everything,' said Quigg, trying to urge Norbert on. 'The Chief will be pleased, and I'll get back in his good books. Not only that, it'll help bring the Burrow Clan together after all the upset of being attacked by the ghosts. A lot of my people were badly shaken. If they see our most important treasure in its rightful place, it'll reassure them that everything's back to normal.'

'Don't you see?' said Gafferty. 'This is so much bigger than keeping your chief happy. It's even bigger than your clan. This affects everyone – all the clans.'

'Why? Trokanis is just one Smidgen. What can he do?'

Gafferty looked back the way they'd come. Trokanis could appear at any moment. There wasn't time for this!

'He's … weird. I mean, scary-weird. And dangerous. I'm not sure why he wants to remake the Mirror but I am sure it's not for anything good. He has magical powers too. I think he was inside my head, controlling me, and he could do the same to you. You can't take him on by yourself. We don't know what he could be capable of!'

'Well, if I get the Great Jewel it won't matter what he's capable of,' said Quigg. 'Because I'll be out of here and back in the Burrow. Now, if I can get this silly rat moving …'

Norbert's nose was twitching anxiously. He glanced upwards and gave a squeal. There was a harsh cry, followed by several more as black, angular shapes descended from above.

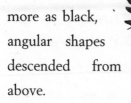

'Crows!' cried Gafferty as Norbert dashed along the alley, ignoring Quigg's commands. Gafferty had forgotten Will's warning about a colony of the birds on the roof of the post office. Now they were attacking! Either they weren't fans of rats, or they thought Smidgens might make a tasty lunchtime snack.

One of the crows spread its claws as it dived and made a grab for Gafferty, scraping the top of her head. She screamed and hit out at the scaly feet above her.

The bird swooped upwards, cawing furiously as a second crow struck. It went to peck at Norbert's face, but the rat came to an abrupt halt, the bird missing its mark and crashing into the wall, its wings splayed out like giant hands. Gafferty and Quigg were both flung to the ground by the sudden stop and rolled across the dusty paving slabs. Another crow dived at them, hopping around the ground in an angry dance, as if it couldn't decide whether it should stab or scratch at its prey. Norbert skittered around in panicked circles, not knowing where to go or what to do without Quigg's guidance.

Gafferty stood shakily and checked her head for blood. Luckily she had only been scratched. Quigg was already on her feet, trying to calm Norbert, reassuring him with soft words so she could climb on to his back. She couldn't see the crow on the ground behind her as it studied her malevolently. There wasn't time for a warning: Gafferty grabbed Quigg's stick out of the girl's hand and launched it at the advancing crow like a spear. It struck the bird in the face and the startled creature launched into the air with a squawk. Quigg turned around in surprise.

'Now *you've* saved *me* in the Smidge of time,' she said. 'I hope you're keeping score of who's saved who.' She leaped on to Norbert and pulled Gafferty up behind her. With a yell she drove the rat on, and they sped down the alley. Gafferty leaned over and picked up Quigg's precious stick along the way. The birds flapped about in the air above them, cursing and squawking and readying for another attack. They swooped as one on the escaping Smidgens, the mass of black feathers blocking out the light. Gafferty screamed again and covered her head with her hands. Then Quigg did the strangest thing: she cheered. A volley of arrows flew from under the archway at the alley's end, their tiny spikes raining down on the birds. The crows swiftly retreated, some with the tiny weapons caught in their feathers.

'Chief Talpa!' cried Quigg.

Half a dozen rat riders emerged from under the arch, each carrying a bow. Gafferty immediately recognised the bearded leader of the Burrow, dressed all in black and riding the biggest rat she had ever seen. The Chief frowned when he saw Gafferty on Norbert's back.

'Thank you for rescuing us, Chief!' said Quigg quickly.

'That was a close thing.'

'I told you not to mix with the Outsiders!' Talpa snapped back. 'If I'd known she was with you, I might have left you to the crows! Interfering troublemakers! Did you deliberately disobey me, girl?'

'No, Chief,' said Quigg. 'I found Gafferty by accident. But she's got important news. You need to hear what she says.'

'It'll be bad news, no doubt!' the Chief said, glaring at Gafferty. 'Trouble follows this one wherever she goes.'

'Please, Chief Talpa, you must hear me out!' begged Gafferty.

'Then make it quick, child. And be thankful that Quigg has spoken up for you, or you'd be crow food.'

Gafferty took a breath. She needed to get this right.

'You know about the power of the Mirror,' she began. 'We share the gift of hearing the voices within the crystal. You're the one who made the connection with our ancestors. You were right.'

The Chief's face softened. Perhaps she was getting through to him.

'What of it?'

'Our ancestors – yours and mine – were there when the Great Jewel was made, when the Mirror was broken far in

70

the past. That past, that event, has come back to haunt the Smidgens once more, and if we don't act together now, then it could be the end of the Smidgens forever.'

'Past? What do you mean?'

'She means there's a Smidgen in that building with the Great Jewel,' Quigg blurted out, pointing at the sorting office. The Burrow Smidgens glanced at each other.

'It's not just a Smidgen, it's Trokanis,' said Gafferty. 'He's still alive and he's after all the pieces of his Mirror. And he needs the piece the Roost took, wherever it is. We have to warn them – he's dangerous, feeding off life force to keep himself young. He knows how to use magic. Even your rat riders might not be a match for him. And the fact that he has the Great Jewel means he's been working with Claudia and her ghosts. We can't take on him and them as well!'

'That's quite a story,' said Talpa. 'What do you think, Quigg?'

Quigg turned and studied Gafferty's face for a moment, struggling to choose between her clan and her new friend.

'I want the Great Jewel back more than anyone, Chief,' said Quigg. 'I want to turn back and get it right now. Gafferty tried to stop me.' She paused for a moment. 'Now, I don't know about magic or anything like that. I'm more of a hit-things-with-stick person than a thinker. But I've learned a bit about people in the past few days, and a bit about myself along the way. And I do know that when Gafferty believes something you have to listen to her. And if Gafferty says *no* then I won't. I trust her. Little people, big heart, as we say. Gafferty has the biggest heart of the lot.'

'And why should we trust you?' asked Chief Talpa. 'Your loyalty to the Burrow has been put in doubt by your actions, girl.'

'Loyalty? This has got nothing to do with loyalty to one clan or the other. This affects all Smidgens! The clans have been divided for too long – we need to work together. And Gafferty and her friends are good people. They care about others and are welcoming to strangers. We've had it wrong for too long.'

Gafferty was taken aback by Quigg's speech. This wasn't the girl she'd first met, hostile and stubborn.

'There isn't time to argue any more!' she said. 'We need to stop all this suspicion and start trusting one another. Otherwise, you'll also never see your Great Jewel again and the whole of Smidgenkind could be in danger. It's time to make your decision, Chief ...'

11

A Little Bird Tells All

Chief Talpa looked at Gafferty as if he were trying to see inside her mind.

'I remember how the Great Jewel affected us both,' he said. 'Our past and future appear to be entwined. You believe it and I feel it too. Something has changed today – perhaps I sensed Trokanis feeding off the Great Jewel. I heard a voice cry out in my head not long ago. There is indeed something greater at work here than clan allegiances.'

Gafferty sighed with relief. It was the first step.

'Come with us to the Roost,' she said. 'Let's bring all the Smidgens together. And then we can act. But we need to go now, as time is running out.'

The Chief nodded.

'We will see what you and the Roost have to say,' he said. 'But I warn you – if you are wasting our time we will leave and be done with you for good.'

He spoke to one of the other Smidgens. 'Mugbo – go back to the Burrow and summon as many rat riders as you can. Make sure they are armed but let them know that the Outsiders are no longer enemies – for now. We shall go on ahead with the Sprout girl.'

Mugbo turned his rat and sped away.

'Well done!' Quigg whispered to Gafferty. 'It was touch and go there for a moment, but you won him around. And you won me around too. For us Burrow Smidgens to give up on getting back the Great Jewel and coming to the Roost just because of something you said … well, it shows we can see the truth in your words, and in your heart.'

'I couldn't have done it without you! You certainly seemed to have changed your opinion of me.'

'Hmmph! It doesn't mean I don't think you're daft, because you are. But daft in a good way, I suppose.'

Gafferty directed the riders to a drain grille nearby. They could use the sewers to get to the Roost without wasting time squeezing their rats through the narrow tunnels of the Tangle. As she clung on to Quigg's mouse-coat, Gafferty had a chance to think through everything she had seen that day. She started to make connections, ideas that had, up until now, just been instincts. Were the voices from the Mirror finally getting through to her, helping her to work out what was going on? She also wondered what would happen when the Burrow and the Roost clans finally met face to face. Could she unite them, or had she just made everything worse?

Noah had been as good as his word. As soon as the school day was over, he had dashed home to contact the Smidgens. He didn't pay any attention to the hearse parked just outside his little house, its occupants hidden behind the tinted glass windows.

'I hope this doesn't take too long,' murmured Mr Ribbons, watching from the driving seat.

'How do you get messages to Smidgens?' mused Totherbligh from the back seat where he and the other ghosts huddled. 'Very small telephones?'

'There, look,' said Claudia, pointing to an upstairs window. Noah had placed a piece of paper against the glass, with a drawing of a bird on it.

'Is that a parrot?' said Hinchsniff. 'Or a weird-looking owl.'

'A cuckoo?' suggested Totherbligh.

'It's a signal, if I'm any judge,' said Claudia. 'A signal for the little bird Smidgens.'

They had to wait for another half an hour, by which time Mr Ribbons was getting testy.

'Are you sure this is going to work?' he growled.

A small shadow darting across the afternoon sky saved Claudia from having to answer. They thought it was a bird at first, but the way it smoothly came to land on Noah's window ledge betrayed the fact that it was a little glider. They watched its tiny pilot unharness himself and tap on the windowpane. Noah's face appeared and he opened the window to let the visitor

in. Claudia slid out of the car's open window and carefully drifted up the wall until she was underneath the ledge.

'I don't believe a word of that ghost's story,' the Smidgen was saying. 'But it's not for me to decide what to do next. I'll have to fly back to the Roost and see what Lady Strigida says.'

'Is there anything I can do to help?' Noah replied.

'Thank you, but you've already been a help. This is Smidgen business and something we'll have to sort out ourselves.'

Claudia heard the pilot clamber out and reattach himself to his glider. She watched as it soared away towards the centre of the town, then she swooped down to the hearse.

'It worked,' she said. 'I'll follow our little bird, and then we can find out where they all nest.'

Mr Ribbons nodded, an unpleasant smile on his face.

Claudia rose back up into the air, keeping an eye on the glider in front. The hearse silently tracked her movements. There were times when it had to divert from Claudia's direct route and follow the path laid out by the streets, and she could feel the invisible tug of her bottle reining her in, but she managed to keep the glider in sight. After a while, she realised it was heading for somewhere that was already familiar to her.

'The hotel!' she said to herself as she watched the glider land in front of the tower's huge window. 'They were there all along right above my head!' She could almost laugh. It was where she had first encountered Gafferty Sprout, one of the smallest and most challenging adversaries she had ever faced. And who, Claudia suspected, might be the only one who could rescue her from her current situation.

She floated gently back to the hearse that had parked in the road outside the hotel.

'They're in the old tower, right at the top,' she said. 'I doubt it's easily accessible to normal humans, so you'll have to rely on us.'

'Very well,' said Mr Ribbons. 'I hope you know what you're doing.'

'What if they don't have the glass?' said Hinchsniff.

'They must have it,' said Claudia. 'We only need to find one more piece and Trokanis said it was right under the Smidgens' noses. It must be in their dwelling.'

'But we can't touch the glass,' said Totherbligh. 'It'll destroy us!'

'We'll force the Smidgens to help us.'

'Hmmm,' rumbled Mr Ribbons. 'There is too much left to chance. I want other options. The Smidgens have a relationship with this Noah boy. They care about him. It could make him useful. We will go and fetch him.'

'He won't cooperate willingly,' said Claudia. She didn't like involving the child. It complicated things.

Mr Ribbons's black eyes flashed.

'I have methods that are very persuasive,' he said.

12

table talk

Will had been keeping an eye out for Gafferty's return from the rafters of the tower. As soon as he spotted the cluster of tiny figures below, he let down several long ropes attached to Upliners, winches that could pull their wearers up a rope without any effort. He couldn't have looked more surprised when he saw who was nervously hanging from Gafferty's shoulders as the winch whisked them to the top of the old tower.

'I wondered if we'd ever see you again,' he said, giving Quigg an awkward hug once he'd dragged her from Gafferty's back. 'I wasn't quite sure if you were really on our side.'

'Get your hands off me, bird boy!' said Quigg.

'Still as friendly as ever, I see,' said Will, rolling his eyes.

'And you're still as stupid,' Quigg retorted, but she gave him a sly grin to show she was joking.

Will was even more surprised when Chief Talpa and a bunch of Burrow Smidgens came up behind them.

'But they think we're the enemy!' he said to Gafferty, as Talpa was helped out of his harness.

'We're all on the same side,' said Gafferty, unbuckling the Upliner with a sigh.

'Not quite,' said Talpa. 'We need to talk to your elders first.'

They clambered through the trapdoor that was the secret entrance to the Roost. The Burrow Smidgens' eyes almost popped out of their heads at the sight of the colourful town.

'This place is amazing!' Quigg said. 'You Roosters certainly know how to live, I'll give you that.'

Will beamed proudly.

'It is brilliant here,' he said. 'We're not all stupid.'

'There's no time for a tour,' said Gafferty. 'We need to find Lady Strigida right away! And where's Crumpeck?'

'He went straight back to his home as soon as we arrived,' said Will. 'He was exhausted from everything that happened, or so he said. He's not come out since.'

They marched to the little house of Lady Strigida, stares from the Roost Smidgens following them the whole way. Nobody tried to stop the fearsome-looking Burrow riders. Gafferty quickly grabbed some food from the market that occupied the attic's floor space. She'd not eaten since breakfast and now it was late afternoon, and she was ravenously hungry. Quigg asked Will to send someone down with some food for the riders' rats, which were resting in the drain outside.

'Gafferty!' Lady Strigida appeared at her front door, looking shocked at the crowd of strangers. 'And this can only be Chief Talpa!'

'He wants to talk,' said Gafferty, her mouth full of cake crumbs. 'He wants to work with us.'

'I'm *thinking* about it,' said the Chief, puffing himself up. He and the old lady eyed each other sternly. Gafferty wondered if they were having a staring competition, but finally Lady Strigida spoke.

'We'd best sit down,' she said. She led them to a table outside the market's inn. She seated herself on one side, with Gafferty, Will and Quigg. Chief Talpa sat opposite with the other Burrow Smidgens.

'I see you've put yourself with the Outsiders,' the Chief said to Quigg.

'It's just a table, Chief. Don't let a piece of furniture get in the way of talking.'

He glowered at her, but before he could reply, Gafferty related her encounter with Trokanis.

'I can hardly believe it!' said Strigida, after Gafferty had finished. 'But I do, for I know you tell the truth, Gafferty, and how could you make up something so strange and so terrible? To think that after all these years Trokanis should still be amongst us, still be capable of malevolence! Thank goodness you're safe.'

'There's something else,' said Gafferty, lowering her voice. 'Trokanis said the last piece of the Mirror is in the Roost, right under our noses.'

'We'll never let him take it!' said Will hotly. 'We'll find it ourselves and we won't let him in.'

'But that's the problem,' said Gafferty. 'I think he might already be here, in a way.'

Strigida's eyes narrowed and she looked at her sharply.

'What do you mean, girl?' she said.

'Isn't it odd that we found Crumpeck wandering around unharmed, after everything that happened? He said he didn't know how he found himself in the Smidgenmoot, which was a bit weird.'

'He was all anxious and bewildered,' said Will. 'It was the exhaustion, that's all.'

'If he was so tired then why did he suddenly dash off home? You had trouble keeping up with him.'

'Speak plainly, Gafferty,' said Strigida.

'I did a lot of thinking on the journey here. And I think Crumpeck knows something. Like where the last piece of the Mirror is. We know we can't trust him when it comes to the Mirror. He's obsessed with finding it. What if he thinks Trokanis is the best hope of finding the pieces and remaking it? What if … he's helping him?'

'I can't believe it!' said Will. 'Crumpeck may be unpredictable, but he's not one of the bad guys.'

'He's connected to the Mirror like I am, and like Chief Talpa. There was a member of each clan there in the Smidgenmoot when the Mirror broke all those years ago. I'm a descendant of the Hive Smidgen – Trokanis said so – and Chief Talpa is descended from the Burrow Smidgen. And I'm certain that Crumpeck's ancestor was there as well. He was affected by the energy from the Great Jewel in the same way as we were.'

'But working with Trokanis?' said Strigida.

'Crumpeck pinches the Great Jewel, then Claudia pinches them both. The next thing we know, we find him unharmed in the Smidgenmoot while Trokanis has the Great Jewel. The common link is Claudia. I think she may have been working for Trokanis too.'

'One of the Big Folk working for a Smidgen?' said Will.

'Trokanis told me as much. He said he used the humans' post system to write letters getting them to do things for him. So why not Claudia?'

'You think Claudia brought Crumpeck to Trokanis along with the Great Jewel,' said Talpa. 'And then Trokanis persuaded Crumpeck to find the last piece!'

'Maybe he used magic to persuade him. Trokanis tried to control my mind, I'm sure of it, and he's been doing the same to Crumpeck.'

Chief Talpa got to his feet, his hands bunching into angry fists.

'Bring that thieving wretch out here!' he bellowed. 'We will take him back to the Burrow, tie him to a golf ball and throw him into the water hazard!'

'You will do no such thing!' Lady Strigida stood up. 'Lay one finger on a member of my clan and—'

Gafferty thumped the table.

'STOP!' she yelled. Everyone looked at her, silenced. 'See how this is dividing us! It's the poison of the Mirror.

And I've a feeling it will only get worse if it's put back together. There was a reason it was broken, a reason the clans worked together to destroy it. It's all to do with the life force that's trapped in the glass. That's what Trokanis really wants. So we have to work together now, before it's too late. The three clans helping each other, the Smidgens united at last. Chief Talpa, Lady Strigida – what do you say?'

13

A Secret in Plain Sight

The two clan elders studied each other across the table. There was a long pause. Who would speak first?

'It appears we have been shown up by a child,' said Lady Strigida finally.

Talpa looked embarrassed.

'She's trouble, all right,' he muttered. 'But she's got a good brain in her head and a gift for talking, I'll give her that. Maybe we need the young to show us past our old, fixed ways.'

He put his hand out across the table. Lady Strigida took it and nodded at Gafferty, who grasped both hands with her own.

'The Smidgens united,' Gafferty said.

Will cheered and the Burrow Smidgens hammered the table with their fists in approval. Gafferty couldn't help smiling. It was the moment she had been waiting for since she had first found her little atlas of the Tangle, abandoned in an old tunnel. The moment when she had decided she would try and find other Smidgens and bring them together so that she would feel a part of something bigger and not quite so alone in the world. With a bit of luck and a lot of effort, her dream had come true.

'One day we will celebrate this moment properly,' said Strigida. 'But only once the danger has passed. Now is the time for action. Bring Crumpeck here.'

A couple of Roost Smidgens hurried to Crumpeck's house to fetch the Smidgenologist. At that moment, Will's older brother Wyn appeared, along with the boys' uncle Abel. Both were frowning.

'You look serious,' said Will after giving Wyn a hug.

'I am,' said Wyn. 'We've been looking for you. I'm glad you're here too, Gafferty.'

'Wyn was one of the afternoon scouts,' said Abel. 'He's just got back from patrol. He's been to see your friend Noah.'

'The human boy?' said Quigg.

'Is he all right?' asked Gafferty.

Wyn nodded. 'But he had some worrying news. The ghosts are back! And listen to this: they want to help us find the bits of the Mirror so we can keep them safe and away from them.'

Gafferty's mouth dropped open in surprise.

'That's the weirdest thing I've heard today,' she said, 'and I've heard some very weird things.'

'We'll worry about that in a moment,' said Strigida. 'It might be that Crumpeck gives us the answers we need, and we won't require any ghostly help at all.'

Crumpeck looked very sorry for himself when he was brought before them. His eyes flicked from one face to another suspiciously.

'Am I on trial?' he said. 'What exactly am I supposed to have done?'

'We just want you to answer some questions honestly,' said Lady Strigida gently.

'Or we'll dangle you from your feet out of that window!' roared Chief Talpa. Crumpeck shook with fright.

'No, please!' he stuttered.

'We will *not* be dangling any Smidgens,' said Strigida, calmly giving Talpa a severe look that only old ladies can do. Talpa folded his arms grumpily as Strigida continued.

'Is it true that you are in league with Trokanis? Did he send you here to find the last piece of the Mirror?'

The Smidgen looked around for an escape but there was none. He was surrounded.

'Trokanis came back for us,' he said weakly. 'All of us. He came back to make the Smidgens great again with his magic. I've read so many books and scrolls of the old times, the wonders the three clans achieved with their creativity, their hard work, their good sense and ... their magic. Only a few individuals had the gift, and they each sought to help their fellow Smidgens. Trokanis was just the same.'

'Except he did something to make them turn against him,' said Gafferty. 'They knew the Mirror he created was bad.'

'Not bad. All magic requires a sacrifice of some sort. That is the nature of power. Trokanis told me that.'

'What sacrifice?' said Gafferty.

Crumpeck stayed silent and looked at his feet.

'Whether you talk or not, Trokanis won't be allowed to remake the Mirror,' said Strigida. 'So you may as well tell us where the last piece is.'

Crumpeck's eyes flashed wickedly, and he smiled.

'I do know where it is …' he said, 'and I don't.'

'Enough of these riddles!' barked Talpa. 'I will play games with this fool no longer. We will find this last fragment ourselves.'

'How, Chief?' said Quigg. 'We don't have a magic glass detector.'

Suddenly a memory crept to the front of Gafferty's mind. She remembered standing by the window the first time she had met Crumpeck. He had been staring at her knife because it was glowing and trembling.

'Yes, we do, Quigg!' she said, leaping up from the table. 'We *do*!'

She ignored their puzzled looks and pulled her knife from her bag.

'The knife reacts whenever it's near another piece of the Mirror,' she explained. 'And I saw it do that over there.' She ran over to the huge window, followed by Will and the others. The late afternoon sun lit up the different coloured pieces of glass and made them shine warmly.

'It's under their noses, he said,' Gafferty murmured, as her knife began to spark and gently quiver in her hand. There, in front of her, was the answer. 'The window! A piece of the Mirror was here all along. All these years it's been right here, where everyone could see it!'

'But which piece is it?' said Will, craning his neck to scan the window in its entirety. 'There's loads of bits to it.'

'Look for another bit that's glowing.'

They all studied the glass sections, trying to spot some telltale sparks or movement.

'There's something strange happening,' said Quigg. 'The window is steaming up. Are we breathing too hard?'

It was something strange, but it wasn't steam. White crystals formed on the window's surface, spreading out in fern-like patterns across the coloured panes.

'Ice,' said Gafferty. 'The window is covered in frost. How can that be? It's summer!'

'Not all the window is covered,' said Will. 'One bit in the centre is still clear.'

They all saw that one lone piece – a piece that shook and flickered – seemed to be repelling the ice, melting it as soon as it could form.

'That's it – the last part of the Mirror!' said Gafferty.

'We've found it! But where did the ice come from?'

'Wherever it came from, it's making the window unstable,' said Abel. 'The glass is cracking! Everybody, stand clear!'

They scurried back to the centre of the tower, chased by the terrible sounds of splintering glass and warping metal. Gafferty, Will and Quigg hugged each other as they watched the huge, beautiful structure collapse, the glass shattering as it fell into a heap of frost-covered fragments.

'I can't believe it's gone!' said Will, tears running down his cheeks. 'I've looked out of that window all my life.'

'On the bright side,' said Quigg, pointing at the glass heap, 'the piece of the Mirror is still intact.'

Gafferty saw that Quigg was right. The piece lay glistening on the top of the pile, unscathed. But no one else saw. Everyone else was staring at the hole left in the wall. Everyone was looking at it with horror. Because that's when the ghosts arrived.

14

The Rout of the Roost

The smoky forms of the ghosts snaked into the attic of the tower, their bodies forming a vortex of mist as they poured through the hole where the window had been. The Roost Smidgens ran in every direction, crying with fear and diving into their houses in panic.

'We've been found!' shouted Abel, helping Lady Strigida away. 'We need to evacuate the Roost!'

'First the Burrow – now here!' yelled Talpa. 'These phantoms are a curse on all Smidgenkind!'

The ghosts swirled around the little town, clouds of malevolence floating over the rooftops. Gafferty couldn't quite make out their different shapes as they intermingled and darted in and out of the houses, but she thought she

saw three different figures. Three? She recognised two of the ghosts, but the third … was it Claudia? Could it be true? She'd become … a ghost! No wonder she didn't have a need for any luggage!

They immediately began their heartless work: stunning the fleeing Smidgens with their freezing touch. Within seconds several small folk fell to the ground, looks of terror fixed on their icy faces. There was chaos as the Smidgens desperately tried to escape from their terrifying pursuers. The Burrow Smidgens had seen this before and attempted to spear their attackers, but it was hopeless; the ghosts merely turned the spears into icicles.

Gafferty, knife still in hand, put herself between the ghosts and her friends.

'Stay back, Totherbligh!' she yelled, as the walrus-like face materialised in front of her. Sparks flew from the glass weapon. Totherbligh had been stung by it before and kept himself safely out of Gafferty's reach.

'Good afternoon, Miss Sprout,' said the ghost, grinning horribly. 'How pleasant to see you again. Found your little birdhouse hidey-hole, haven't we?'

She stabbed at the ghost, but he was too quick and laughed merrily before sailing away to chase some more

Smidgens, who were trying to hide under tables in the market. Others were attempting to leave via the trapdoor, using the Upliners to drop down and out of the tower.

'We need to help get everyone out!' said Gafferty. 'Wyn – lead those Smidgens to the Hive. There's loads of room to spare in our house. Quigg – take the Chief with you.'

'Who put you in charge?' said Quigg. 'What are you going to do?'

'I'm going to grab the piece of the Mirror.'

Gafferty and Wyn sped towards the wreckage of the window. Almost immediately a ghostly shape blocked their path, cornering them against a wall.

'Out of the way, Claudia, if that really is you,' shouted Gafferty, angrily waving the knife. 'I'm sorry you're a ghost but I still don't have time for your nonsense!'

'Gafferty,' hissed Claudia, her expression suddenly earnest. 'We can help each other. You can help me with my … predicament, and I might be able to help you with yours.'

'What? Don't play games, Claudia – just tell us what you want.'

'I know a bit about magic. Life force is the strongest

force in the universe, capable of many things. The power of life force is at the centre of all this.'

Gafferty nodded. That much she had worked out already.

'And? If we get you some life force then you can come back to life, is that what you're saying?' she asked.

'Perhaps. I'm trapped working for a man – an evil creature – who has corrupted life and embraced the sorcery of death. He wants the Mirror for himself. Life force may free me from his servitude. The question is, how do you get it? We know it's in bits of the Mirror. How did Trokanis get it and trap it in the Mirror in the first place?'

'I don't know,' said Gafferty. 'So you're not really helping me at all, are you?'

'I don't have the answers,' said the ghost. 'But if anyone can work this out, it's you, Sprout.'

'I don't believe her, Gafferty,' said Will. 'Even if that was a kind of compliment.'

Claudia encircled them like a wall of cloud.

'A shame,' said Claudia. 'If you don't believe me, I will have to look after myself. Your little thorn of glass might still be useful.'

'Try and take it then,' said Gafferty, creeping forward.

'You know you can't touch it. What are you going to do?'

Claudia growled in frustration. 'Maybe I can't touch the knife, but I can freeze your doubting friend here. And what if I were to accidentally drop him out of the window ... ?'

Will gulped like a goldfish but Gafferty didn't wait to hear any more. She swiped at Claudia with the knife, sending a stream of static from the blade into the ghost, who recoiled instantly with a screech of pain and flew back out of the tower.

'Gafferty!' said Will. 'Look what Crumpeck's up to!'

Taking advantage of the confusion, the old Smidgen had snatched the pane of Mirror glass from the pile of debris and was heading towards what had been the window. Several scout gliders had been left folded up next to it and he grabbed the nearest.

'He's trying to escape!' said Gafferty. 'Will, come on – we must stop him!'

Crumpeck was already on the window ledge. Will quickly strapped himself into another set of wings.

'You're going to have to hang on to me,' he said as they carefully made their way between piles of broken glass. Crumpeck had already taken off and was flying a wobbly route towards the centre of the town.

Gafferty threw her arms around Will's neck, and they jumped straight from the ledge, Gafferty shutting her eyes tightly and holding her breath as they plummeted downwards.

15

The Serpent Strikes

It was a few seconds before Gafferty was brave enough to open her eyes again. She clung to Will for dear life, her heart in her mouth as she watched the street pass by far below them. She could just see Crumpeck ahead of them, trying to keep his glider flying steadily while hanging on to the awkwardly shaped piece of glass.

'We should be able to catch up with him at this rate,' said Will, over the rushing breeze. 'Do you have a plan for when we do?'

'Nope. Rule Four all the way: *if in doubt, make it up.*'

He glanced at her, shame-faced. 'Look, I'm sorry I said I didn't believe you when you said he was up to no good. The truth is, I *did* believe you, but I still wanted to believe there was some good in Crumpeck too.'

'You want to see the good in everyone,' Gafferty said, smiling despite her nerves. 'There's nothing wrong with that. It's one of the reasons you're my friend. And I ... wait, what's that?'

A sleek black shape arched upwards from the ground and came speeding towards them. Gafferty had never seen anything like it. A black serpent soaring through the air, its hollow eyes staring at them, its body made of writhing shadows. Its jaws opened wide as it bore down on them – the thing was going to swallow them whole if they didn't move out of its way. Will tried to swerve but the serpent was travelling too fast.

Gafferty screamed as the creature's mouth engulfed them. They fell into a black tunnel of deathly cold air as if flying through a nightmare made real, the glider spinning around like a leaf in the autumn wind. Suddenly they emerged from the serpent into the sunshine again, but the glider kept spinning, completely out of control and heading straight for the hard concrete road beneath them. It seemed like they had made a habit of tumbling to the earth together, but this time they were going far too fast – there was no way they could ever survive this crash!

Then just at what Gafferty thought was her very last moment, a huge hand seized the glider out of the air. The jolt plucked her arms from Will's shoulders, and she fell again, only to be caught by another waiting hand. She lay on its clammy palm, breathing heavily and looking up at the horrible leering face far above her. It was human, but only just. A round pale face with cold black eyes that matched those of the serpent that had knocked them out of the sky. The very same serpent that was coiled around the man's broad shoulders.

'Well done,' the man said, looking at it like it was a dear pet. The creature dissolved away into nothingness with a soft hiss. 'Not the most elegant solution to a problem, but my *Twilight Worm* spell has often been effective.' He flashed a set of sharp teeth at them. Gafferty shivered. A spell? A Big Folk magic user. Three misty figures faded into view and slithered into three glass bottles that sat on the roof of a large black *kar* parked beside the stranger. The ghosts – this must be the man Claudia said she was trapped by!

'Did you find anything?' the man said, glaring at the bottles coldly.

'No glass, Mr Ribbons,' said Claudia, almost sounding meek. 'But we did find Gafferty Sprout – the girl you have in your hand. She's at the centre of this. She's important. She knows things.'

'You've got the wrong Smidgen!' said Gafferty, trying to sound braver than she felt. 'Crumpeck's just flown off with the final piece of the Mirror and you've stopped us catching him.'

'I see,' said Mr Ribbons, returning his reptilian gaze to Gafferty. 'And what else do you know, I wonder? Where might he be taking the magical crystal? Smidgens are inextricably connected to it, I believe.'

'I don't know!' said Gafferty bluntly. She'd noticed Claudia hadn't mentioned the knife. What did that mean? Was she really wanting to help?

'Oh, dear,' said Mr Ribbons. 'Perhaps you've forgotten. It must be very difficult to remember things when you have such a tiny little brain. It must fill up with thoughts ever so quickly. You really are quite fascinating. Maybe I should dissect this other one to find out how you work.'

He turned to Will, still strapped in his glider, petrified with fear.

'NO!' yelled Gafferty, her heart beating fast and her mind working quicker. 'I do know where there are more pieces of the Mirror. The post office – there's a whole stash of it there.'

'Not any more. We've been there. Trokanis is gone. You'll have to do better than that.'

'Fine,' she said. 'I know of some other crystal, but I'll need to … check some old books to find it.' The lie might give her some time.

'And while you do that,' said Mr Ribbons, 'I'll take care of this little bird.' He dangled the glider between his fat white fingers, letting poor Will swing helplessly underneath. 'Make sure you return soon, Gafferty Sprout. If I get bored, I may be tempted to pluck some of its feathers. Slowly, one by one.'

'No!' she cried, as the man lowered his hand to the ground, tipping her into the dirt. There was nothing she could do except stare at Will's frightened face as Mr Ribbons carried him and the bottles into the *kar*.

'I'll be waiting here,' said Mr Ribbons. 'You have until midnight.' He slid into the driver's seat and closed the door with a slam like a coffin lid.

Gafferty ran as fast as she could to the nearest drain grille and scrambled down into the sewer, tears running down her face. The situation was hopeless! What could she do? She had to rescue Will from that repulsive, evil man, but how? She had no clue where Trokanis or Crumpeck were, no clue where all the bits of the Mirror were. All this chasing around after pieces of glass seemed ridiculous now that Will was in danger. None of it mattered! She fell to her knees in the dark of the pipe and sobbed.

There was a scratching sound from behind her, a pattering of feet, and a rat appeared at her side. She jumped up, startled, but immediately recognised this particular animal. There was someone sitting on its back.

'You look like someone who could do with a bit of help,' said Quigg.

16

Hope

Norbert waited patiently as Quigg jumped from his back and helped Gafferty to her feet. Gafferty buried her face in the girl's shoulder and hugged her tightly.

'What am I going to do?' she cried. 'I've made a mess of everything again. That evil human is holding Will prisoner! He was making horrible threats unless I find the Mirror for him. If only I'd stayed at home like I was supposed to, instead of going on this ridiculous search for the other clans! None of this would have happened.'

'Well, you did go on the search. And it did happen,' said Quigg bluntly. 'But that doesn't make it your fault. You can't stop bad people doing bad things. It's their choice. And lots of good has come out of it too.

You've made loads of new friends and united the clans.'

'It's all for nothing so far.'

Quigg prised Gafferty from her shoulder.

'No, it isn't,' she said firmly. 'After the ghosts disappeared, Strigida took charge of caring for the frozen Smidgens, Chief Talpa and the riders started making a temporary cover for the window, and Wyn and Abel took some young and old Smidgens from the Roost Clan to safety at your home, just in case there's another attack. Talpa and Strigida are heading there too as soon as they can. Everyone was working together, just like you wanted. I found Norbert and tried to follow you and Will. I arrived just in time to hear that human creep talking. He's a dangerous and tricky one, that's for sure.'

'Poor Will! I hate to think of him all alone and afraid.'

'So stop making my collar soggy with your blubbing and think about what we're going to do to set him free instead! There's work to be done and if there's anyone who's good at getting on with things, it's you, Gafferty Sprout. Little people, big heart.'

'Little people, big heart,' Gafferty repeated. It made her feel better.

'We've got until midnight to sort this out, but we're

going to need all the time we can get. Climb aboard Norbert and let's go!'

Gafferty didn't need telling twice.

'Let's go back to the Hive,' she said. 'Talpa and Strigida are there. I need to see my family. And I need to tell Wyn about his brother.'

The rat was soon carrying them through the maze of sewers and drains. Occasionally he would stop and sniff the air before scurrying on. Gafferty's mind was churning with everything she had seen and heard that day, and although she felt weighed down by the fear that things might yet go horribly wrong, she could see two small slivers of hope.

'Trokanis and Mr Ribbons are after the same thing but aren't working together,' she explained to Quigg. 'That could be useful.'

'I don't think having more than one enemy is useful.'

'They're not just our enemies, they're each other's enemies too. If they're busy fighting each other over the Mirror, it might help us get out of a fix. There's something else. Ghost-Claudia seems to be working against Mr Ribbons. She didn't tell him about my knife, so she could really be on our side.'

'She doesn't seem the sort that would be happy

working for somebody else. But you can't trust her, Gafferty. Just because she's working against Ribbons doesn't mean she's on your side.'

Quigg was right, but Gafferty held on to the possibility that Claudia was a secret ally, as that hope was all she had. As they neared the chocolate factory and the sun began to set, the little bit of hope allowed her to think more clearly, and a germ of a plan began to grow.

Dad met them at the door of the house, his Allen key club in his hand and his brow creased with concern.

'When they told me what had happened at the Roost I feared the worst,' he said, giving her a crushing hug.

'They made it here safely!' Gafferty said. 'Thank goodness!'

'I've never seen so many Smidgens crowded around the kitchen table before!'

He led them up the stairs. It was odd, but wonderful, to see the old place looking so busy. As well as Chief Talpa and the Burrow Clan, there were the Roost Clan refugees, including Wyn and his uncle, and, of course, Lady Strigida. Mum somehow found cups for everyone, and Gobkin carried a plate laden with honey cakes around the room in case anyone was hungry. Quigg took three.

Gafferty had to break the awful news of Will being held prisoner to his brother.

'We'll get him back safe and sound, Wyn, I promise,' she said.

He nodded grimly.

'I know we will,' he said. 'We'll do it together.'

'I never thought I'd live to see this day,' said Dad. 'The three clans all in one place. And all thanks to my daughter.'

'It's a proper Smidgenmoot,' said Lady Strigida. 'The first one in centuries. And hopefully, not the last.'

'Let this be an end to our isolation,' said Talpa. 'We have much to learn from each other. It may take some time for trust to grow between us, but it must start

somewhere. Now, Gafferty Sprout, we are putting our trust in you. Tell us what needs to be done.'

Gafferty opened her bag and placed her knife on the table in front of everyone. It shone and sparkled as if it knew it was on show.

'Thanks to Crumpeck, Trokanis now has all the pieces of the Mirror,' she said. 'All except one. This piece – the tiniest piece. He knows I have it. He's waiting for me to bring it to him.'

'What are you going to do, Gaff?' said Mum.

'I'm going to give him exactly what he wants. I'm going to take the knife to him.'

17

Prisoners

Will was thrown roughly into the front passenger seat of the hearse. It was the biggest *kar* he'd ever seen. The black body of the vehicle merged with the dark shadows of the lane so that it seemed to go on forever. Mr Ribbons sank into the driver's seat, as silent as one of his coffins. He never moved unnecessarily, never coughed or sniffed, and, perhaps, didn't even breathe, but his curranty eyes kept an unblinking watch on everything.

'Will?'

Will turned and saw a young boy sat in the back with the bottled ghosts.

'Noah? What are you doing here?'

'They took me from my house,' Noah said miserably.

'They made my family fall asleep. A magic spell or something. They told me that they had followed Wyn from my house to yours. I'm sorry, Will. This is all my fault.'

'It's not,' Will said firmly. 'Don't worry, Noah. We'll sort this out.' He saw that Noah hadn't been restrained. There was no point as there was no way for him to escape. Mr Ribbons might be huge, but he could move fast, and the ghosts were just as quick. 'You've no need to keep him here,' Will shouted up to the undertaker. 'Let him go!'

'I thought a spare prisoner might be useful,' said Mr Ribbons, sounding bored that he had to explain something so obvious. 'Just in case something *bad* happened to my other prisoner.' He gave Will a meaningful look.

Will shivered. What could he do? And what was Gafferty going to do? She would come back for him, he had no doubt about that. She would definitely try and rescue him, so he knew he should stay alert and be ready. He just hoped she would get some help and not rely on her silly Rule Four. How she had got away with that for so long without meeting some horrible death he had no idea. Gafferty had a lot of luck, but it was often luck she had made for herself. That was one of the things he liked about her. But she didn't know that Ribbons had Noah prisoner too. It would be up to Will to make some luck now.

He glanced around the hearse's interior, searching for anything that might help him. He'd only been in one *kar* before and that belonged to Noah's mum. He knew that there were spaces under the seats big enough for a Smidgen to hide in. The dashboard in front of him had a thing called a *raydeeoh* that played the terrible noise Big Folk called music – Noah's mum liked to listen to what he thought was called *kayplop*. He also knew that behind a panel on the dashboard was a thing called a *gluff kompartmint* which Big Folk often used as the *kar*'s rubbish bin and could be full of useful items for a resourceful Smidgen. Noah's mum kept baby wipes, sweets, make-up and spare socks in hers. Will couldn't see Mr Ribbons doing that. He might have dark and horrible things like that Twilight Worm hidden in there.

At the back of the hearse was the large space where the coffin went. It was currently unoccupied, so obviously no dead people wanted a ride to anywhere today. There was a button on the dashboard that was labelled with a little picture of a *kar* with its boot open. There was no way Will was strong enough to pull the handles that opened the other doors, but he might just manage to push that button. It was a possible escape route …

Mr Ribbons shifted in his seat, like a volcano awakening.

'I am unusually impatient,' he rumbled. 'I do not like making deals. I am more used to having my commands obeyed.'

'I'm sure Gafferty will come up with something,' said Claudia from her bottle soothingly. 'She is full of surprises.'

'I do not like surprises either,' said Mr Ribbons. 'That is why I work with death. Death is a certainty, although its manner of arrival may be a surprise.'

'Not for you, master,' pointed out Hinchsniff. 'Death has left you alone for quite some time.'

'I have walked by its side for many years. We are business partners. Death has kept me … alive.'

'In a manner of speaking,' Hinchsniff muttered.

'Gafferty Sprout is not to be trusted,' Mr Ribbons continued. 'She is too clever. I can see it in her eyes. There is too much … *life* in her.'

'We've found her honest, as a rule,' offered Totherbligh. 'Brutally so, to be frank.'

'I still do not trust her. What do you know of the magic glass?' said Mr Ribbons, casting his stony gaze down at Will.

'It's glass,' said Will weakly. 'And magicky?'

'Where would Gafferty Sprout be going to find it? It's a rare, precious thing. Hard to come by.'

'I've no idea,' said Will truthfully. 'I wouldn't tell you if I knew either. Why would I put her in danger?'

If Mr Ribbons was angry, he didn't show it.

'But you might be putting young Noah in danger,' he said, his eyes gleaming, 'if you do not give me the information I desire.'

'Don't tell him anything, Will!' said Noah boldly. 'He's just a bully. Gafferty will be back soon. She'll rescue us both!'

'Quiet, child! Or the first thing I will do when I get my magic glass is make a bottle just for you!'

Will felt sick. Bully or not, neither he nor Noah were in a position to refuse Mr Ribbons right now.

'Please leave Noah alone,' he said to Ribbons. 'Please!'

'Then you must cooperate. Where would Gafferty Sprout go?'

Will had no idea. What could he say?

'Think!' There was a voice, Claudia's, close to his ear. Too quiet for Mr Ribbons to hear. She had sneaked out from her bottle on the back seat. 'It could save all of us! Where would the Mirror be if not in the sorting office?

thoughts. If only Gafferty Sprout had been as easy to manipulate as Crumpeck, things would have gone a lot smoother. Trokanis watched as the old Smidgenologist sorted the pieces of stone, trying to work out how they fitted together when they had once been part of a solid, graceful arch. Back when this place, the Smidgenmoot, had been a hall of wonders. It had been a stroke of luck when Claudia had brought Crumpeck to him. Trokanis had instantly recognised him as the descendant of the Roost Smidgen who had taken a piece of the Mirror all those years ago. Faces stayed strong in Smidgen bloodlines. He had also recognised the hunger in Crumpeck's eyes, the same hunger as his own. Crumpeck was old and didn't like it. He wanted to be young and strong, and the Mirror, with its store of youth-giving life force, was the key. All Trokanis had to do was tell him where the last piece of the Mirror was: hidden in plain sight in the Roost window – unknown even to the Roost Clan themselves. But Trokanis had remembered Crumpeck's ancestor mockingly saying how the glass would look so nice in the tower window, just to add insult to injury.

Now all the pieces were here, back in their home where they belonged. They lay on the stone platform, arranged together to form a circle, reunited once more. The crystals rhythmically glowed pink, then purple, in time to his heartbeat. Sparks flew from their edges and crackled in arcs between them. It was almost as if they were alive. Only a small fragment missing from the centre spoilt the scene.

Suddenly the glass glowed brighter. She was here, just as he had predicted. Gafferty was a clever child. She would see this was the only way.

'Very nice,' said Gafferty, walking slowly down the steps of the arena. 'I see you've made yourself at home.' She tried very hard not to show her nerves. *Don't muck this up, Gafferty*, she thought. *Stick to the plan and leave Rule Four out of it, just this once.*

'I have more right to call this my home than anyone,' said Trokanis with a cold smile. He looked younger than the last time she had seen him. He'd obviously been using some more of the life force from the crystals. 'I knew you would come here eventually, Gafferty. I just had to wait. And I am good at waiting. I assume you have brought your knife with you?'

'Perhaps.' Gafferty circled the platform warily. 'Or

maybe I threw the knife in the river. What would you do then?'

'Except you haven't, have you? It's there in your bag, as it always is. You're here because you know this is destined to happen. The timings of these events cannot be coincidence. The Mirror is to be remade. A new age will dawn for the Smidgens.'

'A new age for you, you mean! A younger age and one that lasts forever, once you've had your fill of all that life force.'

'It needs my magic to work, and in return I benefit, that is correct. But think of how this will aid the Smidgens. No more hunting and scavenging in secret. No more hiding. The Mirror will transport you with a thought. You could travel beyond the town – haven't you ever wondered what lies in the Big Outside?'

She hesitated. It was like he was reading her mind. Was that part of his ability to manipulate people, to control their thoughts? She'd craved freedom right from the start of this adventure, freedom to explore and make new friends. It was what had set her on this path. Seeing the world had become her dream, once she had realised there was a world out there to see.

'Just with a thought?' she said.

'Just with a thought.'

She moved closer to where the fragments of the Mirror lay. They were getting agitated, sensing the knife. She could hear the voices echoing from within them but this time they were louder and clearer. Crumpeck turned towards her. He could hear them too. They were starting to make sense, warning her: *Don't do this! Stop now!*

She ignored them.

'I'll give you the knife,' she said. 'In return, I want to be the first to use the Mirror. I want you to promise that I will be the first.'

Trokanis raised an eyebrow but showed no other emotion. What was he thinking? Was he wondering if this was a trick, or was he plotting a trick of his own?

'Very well,' he said, after a moment. 'I promise. Put the knife with the other pieces.'

Gafferty laid the blade on the platform, trying to block out all the desperate cries from the other fragments. The glowing lights glowed ever brighter until the whole of the vast chamber was filled with an intense pink-and-purple radiance. With a crackle of sparks, the pieces of the

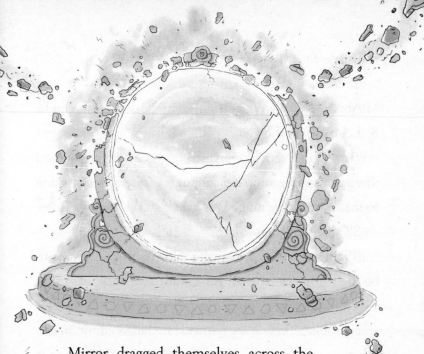

Mirror dragged themselves across the stone, moving towards each other, re-forming the circle until only the spiderweb of a break between them remained.

Trokanis raised a hand and the pile of rubble at Crumpeck's feet rose into the air. The stones flew about the platform, spinning, rotating and fitting together, a jigsaw puzzle completing itself until within seconds the Mirror's frame had been recreated, an arch the size of a Smidgen door.

'Now the last spell, the final magic needed to remake the Mirror stronger than before,' said Trokanis. 'I need your help for this, Crumpeck.'

Crumpeck scampered to his side.

'Whatever you want, master,' he said, his eyes bright with anticipation.

Trokanis seized him by the shoulder, gripping him tightly. Crumpeck looked at him, confused, and tried to move away but found he was frozen to the spot. Gafferty could only stare in horror as Trokanis's eyes shone purple and lightning poured from his fingers into Crumpeck's body. Crumpeck opened his mouth as if to scream, but only a wheezy croak came out as his face began to wrinkle and his limbs began to wither. His beard grew longer, thinner and whiter. Gafferty had thought of Crumpeck as an old man before, but now he was an antique! He sank to the floor, too frail to stand, his tortoise-like face full of confusion.

'Thank you, Crumpeck,' said Trokanis. 'You have served your purpose. Now the moment I've been waiting centuries for is finally here …'

19

A Voice from the Past

Trokanis pointed a finger at the broken Mirror. Purple lightning poured out once more, this time engulfing the fragments of glass. They began to bond with each other, the crack shrinking more and more until it had completely disappeared.

'The Mirror is remade,' said Trokanis, his eyes fading back to their normal colour.

'What have you done to Crumpeck?' Gafferty yelled. 'You've turned him into a fossil!'

'The spell was powerful. It required an infusion of life force. Where else was I to obtain it? I certainly wasn't wasting any of my own. Crumpeck's lucky I didn't take it all.'

'You're a monster! A horrible heartless … thing! He doesn't deserve that after all he's done for you. No Smidgen would ever do something so terrible to another. You're not one of us.'

Trokanis was unmoved. 'I was cast out long ago. Your words are of no consequence.'

He raised his hand and the perfect circle of the Mirror rose from the platform and sailed between the two arms of the stone arch. It hung there on unseen supports, a window floating in the air. Its centre shone with pale white light edged with pink. Trokanis turned to Gafferty.

'I made a promise to you. The Mirror is ready. Do you wish to use it or not?'

Gafferty was still reeling from what she'd seen. Could she trust this creature? What was stopping him from draining all the life out of her too?

'Hurry, Gafferty. My patience is limited.' Trokanis let a blast of lightning fly from his fingers and strike the ground nearby. That was worrying. As well as getting younger, his powers seemed to have increased too.

Then she remembered: Will's safety depended on her and she couldn't turn back now. She swallowed hard and stepped up to the Mirror.

'Yes. I do want to use it. How does it work?'

'Face your reflection and imagine the place you wish to go to. Then step forward. The Mirror will do the rest.'

'And how do I get back?'

'Say the word *Reverto* and you will return to this spot. You can only bring the things you carry and cannot bring anyone with you.'

Trembling with fear, she did as she was told. She saw her own scared face looking back at her, her eyes red with exhaustion. She also saw anger and a determination to make sure Trokanis got what he deserved. *Keep calm*, she said to herself, *and let's do this*. She focused all her thoughts on her destination. Then, taking a deep breath, she walked towards the shimmering glass.

The Mirror shivered and she saw the glass melting around her like liquid silver. It enclosed her completely, as if she were sinking into a pool of light. A strange tingling sensation ran up and down her body like hot pins and needles. For a moment she thought she would drown in the strange mirror substance, but she quickly realised she was breathing normally. The liquid glass gently released her from its grip. She looked around. This wasn't where she'd expected to be. It hadn't worked! Trokanis had lied to her after all – either that or the Mirror was still broken.

She was standing in a room filled with books. They completely covered the windowless walls. Volumes bound in coloured cloth with gold lettering on their spines were everywhere. Lamps lit the room, making it feel cosy and welcoming, but there was something not quite right about the place. It felt unreal, some kind of ghostly vision. It also felt familiar. Just then she realised she wasn't alone.

A Smidgen sat at a desk nearby, a woman writing busily in a book. She looked up at Gafferty sadly.

'You're here,' the woman said. 'I hoped I wouldn't see you, Gafferty.'

'How do you know me?' Gafferty replied. 'Who are—?' She stopped. She recognised the woman's face. It was like her own. 'Are we related?'

'My name is Relanna.'

'Relanna … Relanna Sprout! You're my ancestor. But you lived hundreds of years ago! How are you … ?'

The woman smiled kindly.

'I am not a ghost. But I am not alive either. I died long, long ago. What you see … is a remnant. The piece of my life force stolen by Trokanis and locked into the Mirror. You're inside the Mirror with me now.'

'But I'm supposed to be somewhere else.' Gafferty began to panic. 'Trokanis tricked me!'

'No, he didn't. This is my doing. I've diverted you from your journey, just for an instant. Time works differently here. This is all happening in the blink of an eye, even though it may feel longer to you.'

'I don't understand.'

'That is why I brought you here. So I can explain. The Mirror is a thing of evil. That is why it was destroyed. Trokanis persuaded the Smidgen clans that with the Mirror he had created an object of great magic, and he had. We accepted it gratefully and made much use of it. But then we discovered its true purpose.'

Gafferty sat down at the desk in front of Relanna.

'It's about life force, isn't it?' she said. 'I've had an inkling before now, but after what I've just seen I know it's true.'

Relanna nodded.

'Every time a Smidgen passed through the Mirror some of their life force was stolen. Not enough for them to notice, but with each journey they took their life's energies were being slowly drained.'

'That pins-and-needles feeling I just had – the Mirror was doing it to me too!'

'Yes. But don't worry. You are young, filled with potential and full of life, so it wouldn't have harmed you.

The life force Trokanis stole was being used to extend his own lifespan and increase his magical abilities. We didn't notice at first, but then after a while we realised that those of us who used the Mirror the most were aging the fastest. Meanwhile, Trokanis didn't age, and even began to get younger.'

'It's awful!' Gafferty's fists clenched in rage. 'So you broke the Mirror to stop him and separated the pieces.'

'Yes. And the clans went their separate ways too. We had been distracted by our greed and desire for an easy, selfish existence. Life became more of a struggle after that. Smidgen society crumbled. And while the Mirror was broken, it still contained power. Some of the unused life force was trapped in the pieces. My own and others. It was our voices you've been hearing, trying to warn you.'

'Except it wasn't until the Mirror was put together that I could understand you. I know the Mirror's dangerous, but I need it to work, just this once, and then I'll destroy it too. For good.'

'I fear that may not be possible, but if anyone can find a way it is you, Gafferty Sprout. You have achieved so much already. Destroy the Mirror for good and finally we will be able to rest.'

Gafferty nodded. Then she noticed the book Relanna had been writing in. She'd seen it somewhere before.

'The atlas of the Tangle!' she said. 'You're the Smidgen who made it! And this place is the abandoned library I found it in. You've been helping me right from the start.'

Relanna smiled. She was beginning to fade.

'The Hive Clan are so proud of you, Gafferty. And so are your family ...'

'I know,' said Gafferty. 'I just hope I can live up to it.'

20

The Smidgens Strike Back

FWOOM!

A flash of brilliant white light filled the hearse and lit up the entire lane. Mr Ribbons roared with outrage, his tiny black eyes momentarily blinded.

'What is happening?' he thundered. 'This is magic! I can sense it! Who dares to assault me with this sorcery?'

Will was knocked off his feet by the burst of energy. Claudia, by now back in her bottle on the rear seat, rolled around inside it like laundry in a tumble dryer. The other two ghosts squealed in shock and Noah covered his eyes.

'What's going on?' said Totherbligh.

'It's an ambush!' screeched Hinchsniff.

A tiny circular doorway had appeared in the air inside the car.

'It worked!' were the first words Gafferty said as she half fell, half jumped from the magical doorway and landed on the passenger seat. 'Trokanis was telling the truth after all.'

The doorway shrank to a dot behind her, and the light faded. Gafferty saw Will, lying on his back and looking up at her in wonder.

'Gafferty?' he said.

'Are you all right? I came as quick as I could.'

'That's quite an entrance,' he said, rubbing his eyes as

she pulled him upright. 'Even by your standards. How did you do that?'

'No time to explain – we need to go! I can't take you back the same way, unfortunately.'

'We can't go, Gafferty – they've got Noah too!'

'Gafferty – I'm here!' Noah called from the back seat.

'No!' Gafferty turned pale. 'I had everything planned this time. You know what this means ...'

'Rule Four?'

'Rule Four. Let's get off this seat!'

Mr Ribbons let out a growl like an animal.

'Nobody is going *anywhere*!' he said.

Gafferty dragged Will down into the gap between the passenger seat and the door just as Mr Ribbons's massive fist landed on the cushion, punching a hole right through its stuffing.

'You will regret this, Gafferty Sprout!'

They scrambled to safety in the darkness under the seat. Gafferty gestured to Will to stay silent, then reached into her bag for her rope and pin hooks. Then she clambered back up on to the cushion. Before Ribbons could react, she flung one of the hooks as high as she could. Gafferty's luck was on her side as the hook caught in the switch for the *raydeeoh*. She pulled with all her might – turning the *raydeeoh* on – and then jumped off the seat, dragging the button around even more as she swung from the line. The switch also controlled the *raydeeoh* volume and Gafferty had turned it up to maximum.

Music suddenly blasted out at full volume, making the hearse vibrate and rattling the windows.

'You wretched creatures!' yelled Mr Ribbons over the noise. 'Vermin! Parasites!' He reached under the seat, his hands desperately grasping for the hidden Smidgens. That was when things really started happening.

When Gafferty had said she had a plan she had meant it! She'd come a long way from relying on Rule Four. Not long after she had returned to the Hive, the rat riders of the Burrow had arrived, led by Mugbo. One rider was sent to keep watch on the hearse, while a Roost scout glider kept a discreet surveillance from the skies. As soon as Gafferty left for the Smidgenmoot, more and more Smidgens had joined them. Little did the occupants of the hearse realise they were now completely surrounded.

The music was the signal the clans had been waiting for. Immediately the hearse came under attack. Hundreds of small, dark objects began hailing down on the car's windscreen, exploding as they found their target and spreading a thick gooey substance over the window.

'Now what?' said Mr Ribbons, who had at last found the *raydeeoh*'s off switch. A flock of Roost Clan gliders were swooping down from the buildings above the lane, each dropping one of the little missiles as they passed overhead.

'What are they?' said Will, peeping out from under the seat.

'Fondant-filled chocolate eggs!' said Gafferty with a giggle. 'We "borrowed" them from the chocolate factory. He won't be able to see out of his *kar* for a while. That stuff is going to be a nightmare to clean off, never mind all the dents they'll leave in the bonnet!'

'Do not think you can stop me!' snapped Mr Ribbons. 'I will not be intimidated by some ghastly little insects!'

He opened the door and heaved himself out, shaking his fist at the gliders. Claudia left her bottle and oozed under the seat where Gafferty and Will were hiding.

'Quickly!' she hissed. 'Now's your chance to escape! You can sneak past him.'

'Not without Noah!' said Will. 'We can get him out of the back if you press that button on the dashboard.'

'Now who's using Rule Four?' said Gafferty. 'Good thinking, Will.'

Claudia nodded and extended a cold hand to the boot

door button. The back of the car opened with a quiet *clunk*.

The two Smidgens ran under the seat to where Noah was crouched, looking bewildered by the noise and chaos around him. As soon as he saw them, he grinned with relief.

'Let's get out of here!' said Gafferty.

Noah quickly lifted them on to his shoulders and began to climb over the back seat and into the coffin compartment, as Totherbligh and Hinchsniff watched from inside their bottles. He carefully lifted the back door of the hearse and climbed down on to the road. He peered around the side of the car, keeping himself hidden. Mr Ribbons was standing in the middle of the street. The gliders of the Roost were circling him, diving downwards to buzz his head like an annoying swarm of gnats. The man raised his hands into the air and began chanting words in some unknown, foul-sounding language.

'What's he doing?' said Will.

Before Gafferty could answer, the black serpent melted into the air at Mr Ribbons's shoulder.

'The Twilight Worm!' gasped Gafferty. 'He's going to use it to attack the gliders ...'

21

A Desperate Plan

'We have to do something!' said Will. There was a scrabbling sound from somewhere near Noah's feet and a voice called up to them:

'Don't worry, bird boy! We've got it covered.'

A rat scurried out from under the hearse, carrying Quigg on its back, her face unusually cheerful. Behind her were Chief Talpa and lots more Burrow Smidgens, armed and ready for action. Even Quigg had a spear instead of her pointy stick. Noah's jaw dropped in amazement at the sight of the tiny army.

'You're so much better than action figures,' he said.

'You did it, Gafferty!' said Will. 'You united the Smidgens. All the clans are working together.'

They were just in time. Mr Ribbons unleashed the Twilight Worm, sending it flying through the squadron of gliders, swatting them like flies. It took all their pilots' skill to stop them plummeting to the ground.

'Charge!' yelled Chief Talpa, and raced towards him, followed by ten other rats and their riders, including Quigg. The rats jumped on the man, biting and scratching his legs, and one even crawled up his trouser leg. Mr Ribbons screamed with horror and leaped around the lane, trying to shake off the offensive animals.

'Get them away from me!' he squealed. Distracted by the attack, he lost all concentration – and control – over the spell. His magically created monster disintegrated into nothingness as quickly as it had been conjured. Quigg and Norbert came scurrying back to the hearse.

'That'll teach him!' she said.

'Now we need to get you away from here, Noah,' said Gafferty. 'And then we can get back to the Smidgenmoot.'

'But Mr Ribbons knows about the Smidgenmoot,' said Will. 'I'm sorry, Gafferty. He forced me to tell him. But I didn't tell him where it was.'

Gafferty frowned for a moment. Then she said:

'Noah – do you think you could be brave and help us

at the same time? It would be just like being a secret agent on a mission.'

Noah's eyes lit up and he nodded. He'd always wanted to be a secret agent.

'We need you to lead Mr Ribbons to the Smidgenmoot. Not too fast, but get him to the toy shop. The Smidgenmoot is underneath it.'

'Why?' said Will. 'Isn't that the last place we want him?'

'If we're going to help Claudia – and I think we should – then we need him there. Trust me. Some of the riders can go with Noah and keep him safe and the Roost can keep a lookout from above. Ribbons will follow, thinking we're with him.'

Quigg stuck her spear in the nearest tyre of the hearse. There was a satisfying hiss as the tyre began to deflate.

'I'm just making sure he doesn't go anywhere too quickly,' she said with a mischievous grin.

A group of riders were given their instructions. Meanwhile, Mr Ribbons had managed to rid himself of the last rat and dived back into the car, locking the door behind him. As soon as he was in the hearse, Noah and his escort hurried down the lane. There was a roar from inside the *kar*.

'Mr Ribbons has discovered he's lost his prisoners!' said Gafferty. 'Let's go! Noah can do the rest, and hopefully Claudia will help.'

Gafferty clambered on to Norbert's back behind Quigg, while Will had the honour of riding behind Chief Talpa. He gave a wave to the Roost Smidgens who were still circling overhead. The rats galloped back into the drain.

'Thank you for coming back for me, Gafferty,' said Will. 'And using the Mirror too! But that means ... Trokanis has your knife!'

Gafferty nodded grimly.

'All I wanted to do when I gave him my knife was for him to remake the Mirror so I could use it to get to you,' she said. 'Mr Ribbons could have all sorts of powers we don't know about. It was the best way I could think of getting inside the *kar* quickly and taking him by surprise.'

'It certainly did that!'

'I probably could have rescued you by myself, of course, but I was glad to have the other clans helping out.'

Will grinned.

'I always knew you'd come back for me,' he said.

'You've been by my side through most of this daft

adventure. It's only right that we finish this together.'

'Do you think we can stop Trokanis?'

'I'm not sure. The only thing I'm sure about is that we have to try.'

When they knew they were close to the huge meeting chamber, they slowed their pace and crept cautiously, as if they were approaching a dangerous animal in its lair. Rounding a corner, they found Dad, Lady Strigida, Wyn and his uncle, and a group of armed Smidgens, quietly waiting. They were overjoyed to see Will safe and sound, and that Gafferty's plan to use the Mirror had been successful.

'We couldn't have done it if we hadn't worked together,' said Gafferty. 'If there was any proof that the Smidgens should be united, this was it.'

'Do you have a plan for what to do next, my clever daughter?' asked Dad. Gafferty realised that he wasn't joking. He was beaming with pride.

'Actually, no,' she said awkwardly. 'And it could get complicated when Mr Ribbons shows up. Or it could help. Either way, there's magic involved in this. Trokanis is strong and he's shown he's not afraid of hurting people to get what he wants.'

'Where do we start?' said Abel.

'The Mirror is the key,' said Gafferty. 'Destroy that and he'll have no way to feed himself.'

'But then we're just back to where we started,' said Wyn. 'What's to stop him putting the fragments together again?'

'If we can imprison him and keep him away from any bits of glass, then eventually time will catch up with him,' said Dad. 'He'll get what's coming to him in the end.'

The Smidgens all looked at each other uncomfortably, but there didn't seem to be any better ideas.

'We'll divide ourselves into two groups,' said Strigida finally. 'One group will try to distract Trokanis and keep him busy, while the other will focus on destroying the Mirror.'

'But don't let Trokanis touch you,' warned Gafferty. 'Unless you want to end up a hundred and ninety years old, or worse, as a pile of dust. And don't look too long in the Mirror either, otherwise you'll end up Smidgen-knows-where.'

With grim faces, they made their way through the tunnel towards the Smidgenmoot, led by Gafferty, Will and Dad. They silently crowded around the entrance to the chamber, hiding in the shadows. Gafferty peeked around the doorway. Trokanis stood in the centre of the platform, bathed in the glow of the Mirror. It floated serenely in its frame, shimmering and flickering like a huge unblinking eye. Crumpeck, feeble and helpless, sat on the ground nearby.

'It's so beautiful,' whispered Will from behind her shoulder.

'Don't be fooled,' said Gafferty. 'Beautiful and powerful but completely evil.'

'The Distraction Group will go first,' whispered Abel. 'Then the Destruction Group will follow once Trokanis's focus is elsewhere. We don't want to give him a chance to work out what's happening. Are we ready?'

Everyone nodded. Gafferty, Quigg, Will and Wyn were all in the Distraction Group, along with the younger, faster Smidgens. Dad and the other bigger and bulkier Smidgens like Chief Talpa were in the Destruction Group. Lady Strigida would get Crumpeck to safety.

'Whatever happens in there, Gafferty,' Dad said, his eyes glistening, 'your mum and me couldn't be prouder of you and everything you've achieved. Mum would be here too if she and Gob weren't sorting out all the refugees with food. You deserve to be the Head of our Clan, the Chief of the Hive, because we'd both follow you to the ends of the world.'

He threw his arms around her and buried her in his chest as if he didn't want to let go.

'We'll be fine, Dad,' was all she managed to say. He gently released her, and she could see the tears on his cheeks. *Please, please let Dad come out of this all right,* she said to herself.

Abel gave the signal. The Distraction Group tiptoed into the chamber and, keeping to the shadows, silently moved around the edge of the platform. The Destruction Group could only wait, ready to slip into the cavern and creep around the other way, putting the Mirror between them and Trokanis. When the Distraction Group had gone as far as they could, Abel nodded at Gafferty. This was it. This was the moment. Gafferty took a deep breath.

'LITTLE PEOPLE, BIG HEART!' she roared, and they charged.

22

Trokanis's Triumph

Trokanis turned sharply around at the noise. A look of disdain appeared on his face at the sight of the crowd of Smidgens running towards him.

'What a scruffy mob!' he said with a laugh. 'The years really have seen a downturn in the fortunes of the Smidgens. It's a good thing I came back when I did.' Then he saw Gafferty at their head. 'The Mirror worked, I see.'

'And for the last time!' said Gafferty. 'We're going to put an end to your ways, using your own kind as some sort of snack bar! We're going to lock you up for good and it'll only be porridge that you'll be tasting from now on.'

They surrounded him, careful to keep out of arm's reach.

'Is that so?' taunted Trokanis. 'And who will be the first to try and take me?'

Wyn jumped forward before anyone could stop him and looked like he was about to grab the ancient Smidgen.

'No, Wyn!' called Will.

Trokanis was too quick. He raised his hands and fired bolts of purple lightning from his fingertips at the boy. Wyn yelped in pain and fell to the ground, the sparks playing around his stricken body.

'Wyn!' said Will, and ran to his side. For a moment, Gafferty thought Wyn might suffer the same fate as Crumpeck, but he seemed unharmed, just slightly stunned.

'I don't think he's going to try and hurt any of us too much, if he can help it,' she told Will. 'We're too useful to him, especially the younger Smidgens. Who else is going to provide him with new life force?'

'It's so horrible!' said Will, cradling Wyn's head. The other Smidgens tried to close the circle around Trokanis but didn't dare get nearer.

There were yells from the other side of the arena as the Destruction Group rushed forward to attack the Mirror, led by Dad. He raised his metal club over his head and brought it down on the Mirror's delicate face with all his considerable might. The club hit the glass with a huge *CRACK!* that shook the Mirror so that it wobbled violently in its frame. Sparks showered from its surface, cascading on to the black stone floor.

'Take that, you poor excuse for a windowpane!' Dad said triumphantly. He stood back to admire his handiwork, but his face quickly dropped. There was no sign of any damage whatsoever. In fact, the Mirror was completely unmarked.

'That can't be!' said Dad. 'I've broken rocks with this club. How can a piece of glass survive that?'

Then Chief Talpa and the other Smidgens were each taking it in turns to strike the glass with hammers and sticks and metal bolts. Nothing, neither tool nor weapon, had any effect.

Trokanis, still surrounded, smirked at the futile attempts to damage his creation.

'Did you really think I would make the same mistake twice?' he said. 'How could I let my precious Mirror, the result of years of work and magical craft, be broken again? I've spent centuries waiting and planning for this moment. I wasn't going to let anyone get in the way this time. When the pieces were fused, I bound in a spell of protection. Nothing can break the Mirror from the outside.'

'What are we going to do?' said Dad, looking around at the others.

'You will do nothing,' stated Trokanis. 'You cannot attack me, and you cannot destroy the Mirror. You might as well face it: I have won.'

'You will never win against us!' said Strigida, who was by Crumpeck's side. 'Look at us. Look how we stand together – all three clans, our differences put aside. We are Smidgens united!'

'We'll find a way!' yelled Gafferty. 'Even if there's only one of us left to stand against you.'

'Admit defeat, Sprout. Then we can happily co-exist. We can work together. I'm not asking much of any of you. Think of all the possibilities the Mirror holds for the clans – the ability to travel far and wide with only a thought. You've experienced it yourself and have come out unharmed. Why would you stop others doing the same?'

The Smidgens all looked at Gafferty. She'd used the Mirror, so what was the problem with anyone else having a go? It seemed quite reasonable and a lot less effort than fighting. Gafferty sensed fear was getting the better of them, or was it Trokanis's mind games? She sighed heavily and walked up to him, so that she was dangerously close to his death grip.

'It's been a very long day,' she said, looking him straight in the eye. 'I've been chased by rats, attacked by crows and flying snakes. I've been threatened several times, and by people far more frightening than you, Trokanis. I've seen my friends and family in danger. And I've had some of my life force stolen from me. Unharmed, perhaps, but only for now. We know what you are, Trokanis: a selfish, desperate thief. And we won't stop fighting you until we have justice. We, the Three Clans, are united in that.'

Any hesitation vanished. All the Smidgens lifted their weapons and let out a cheer that echoed around the Smidgenmoot, a sound that had not been heard there in centuries and which shook its very walls.

'A pretty speech,' sneered Trokanis, over the rumble of noise. 'But it still doesn't change anything. I am more than a match for you and the Mirror cannot be broken whatever you try.'

However, no one was listening. The shaking of the Smidgenmoot's walls, instead of fading away, was increasing, the rumbling getting louder. Rocks and dust began to fall from the ceiling high above, and cracks appeared, spreading like tree roots from one side to the other.

'It's an earthquake!' said Talpa, as the ground trembled under their feet.

'It can't be – not here!' said Strigida, but the whole chamber shook again as if in answer. The Smidgens, all except Trokanis, ran for the tunnels as an enormous fissure opened in the ceiling and light poured into the cavern, even though it was night. Huge boulders tumbled down to the floor and smashed into a hundred pieces just where Gafferty and Will had been standing moments before. Then the roof began to rise. An evil-looking black smoke surged into the Smidgenmoot through the fissure and formed a pair of giant claws. Its nails dug into the rock and pulled the roof upwards, opening the Smidgenmoot like a pie with its crust being ripped off. All the while, Trokanis stood his ground next to the Mirror, even as rocks crashed and splintered around him.

'What's happening?' said Will, as they crouched near the doorway. 'Is this Trokanis's doing?'

'No!' said Gafferty, pointing to the hole where the ceiling used to be. 'Look! Noah's completed his mission!'

A huge shadow loomed over the now open chamber, silhouetted against a bright electric light.

'Who?' said Dad. 'Is that one of the Big Folk?'

'Worse than that,' said Gafferty. 'It's Mr Ribbons!'

23

The Hand of Darkness

'A nest of insects!' bellowed the undertaker, looking down on them menacingly. Behind him they could see a spacious room filled with boxes. It was the storeroom of the toy shop! Nobody would be there at night-time so it would have been easy for him to break in. Noah, scared but unharmed, peeped over the crater's edge. Gafferty sighed with relief. She could see rat riders were hiding behind the boxes – they could whisk him away if things got bad.

'So this is where you hide,' Mr Ribbons was saying. 'Under the playthings of a children's shop! I shall make playthings of you all!'

In one hand he gripped the three glass bottles, the

trapped ghosts looking on from inside their prisons. The other hand he waved over the cavern and muttered some strange words. More enchanted smoke appeared, this time black serpents and other monsters who swirled around the Smidgenmoot, spreading a deathlike cold and making the Smidgens shiver with terror. Some lost their nerve completely and ran back down the tunnels.

'We can't fight this and Trokanis!' said Abel. 'We should retreat – and quickly!'

'Wait!' said Gafferty.

Mr Ribbons had noticed the Mirror. His beady eyes lit up and his black tongue ran over his sharp teeth hungrily.

'Stay back!' shouted Trokanis at the man. 'Your business with me is complete. You have your bottles back!'

'Ah, the tiny wizard!' laughed Mr Ribbons. 'I should have kept you as a pet. You were not telling me everything about your little bits of glass, were you?'

'They are not your concern!'

'All magical glass is my concern, especially if it does what my ghost here informs me it does. I will take it for my collection.'

From inside her bottle Claudia smiled at Gafferty. *I hope we're thinking along the same lines*, Gafferty thought.

Mr Ribbons dismissed the smoke creatures and reached down into the Smidgenmoot, his fat white fingers stretching out for the Mirror.

'No!' Trokanis looked horrified. He saw the result of all his long efforts, his very life being taken away from him. He frantically fired his purple lightning into the man's hand. Mr Ribbons swiftly withdrew it as if he'd been stung by a wasp.

'How dare you!' he roared. 'How dare you think your puny pixie magic is any kind of match to my necromancy! You shall pay for your impertinence.'

Black smoke belched from his fingertips and poured over the Smidgen, covering him from head to toe. The other Smidgens, watching from nearby, heard a scream from within the seething fog as it twisted around him, more and more, so that he completely disappeared inside a cocoon of darkness.

'We should do something!' said Will. 'Help him!' Wyn put his hand on his brother's shoulder and shook his head.

'You wished to live forever!' Ribbons cried. 'Then you shall! You will remain in this rat hole where you belong for all time!'

The cocoon carried Trokanis to the wall of the cave

and spread tendrils of smoke over the rock. The wall opened like a cage and Trokanis was dragged inside it. There was one last scream before the stone closed around him, sealing him into the rock for good. As the smoke cleared all trace of Trokanis was gone.

There was no time for the Smidgens to take in what had happened before Mr Ribbons was reaching for the Mirror once more. His fingers stroked its surface, and it released a shower of white sparks as if it were trying to resist his touch. But Mr Ribbons was deadly serious. Nothing was going to stop him now. He plucked the Mirror from the stone arch and drew it up to his face to examine it more closely. His greedy eyes ran over its polished exterior, admiring its smoothness and studying his reflection in the magical glass.

'Yes,' said Gafferty to herself. 'Go on, Mr Ribbons. Look in the Mirror with your horrible dead eyes. Let's see what happens when it tries to steal life force from someone who doesn't have any.'

Something was definitely happening. As he gazed at himself, Mr Ribbons seemed to be giving off more of the sinister black smoke, but instead of escaping through his fingers as a spell it was seeping from his skin in wafts. The man watched curiously as the smoke was sucked into the

Mirror. It wasn't his doing; it was the Mirror's. It was trying to take the life force from him, trying to make him pass through it. It drew more and more of the smoke from him, faster and faster.

Mr Ribbons suddenly began to look worried. He pulled the Mirror away from his face and was about to dash it to the ground. At that moment the ghosts pounced. They flew from their bottles and wrapped themselves around Ribbons's hand and wrist, even though it brought them close to the Mirror and its fatal energy. Their combined touch froze the man's hand and fingers so that he was unable to let go of the Mirror, forced to look at it as it pulled the magic out of him.

'What are you doing?' he screeched. 'You are my servants! Unfreeze me or I will make you pay!' The ghosts said nothing and watched. Noah backed away, keeping his distance.

Mr Ribbons was frightened, something he hadn't experienced before. He howled as the magic left him, more and more, faster and faster. The Mirror began to glow and tremble in his hand as if it couldn't stop what was happening, as if the whole terrible process was out of control. Ribbons's face began to twist as the Mirror tried to draw his huge bulk inside it. The Mirror began to shake violently. Then … it imploded.

24

Second Chances

The noise was terrible. Mr Ribbons screamed as he was stretched and twisted, and dragged into the Mirror as it collapsed in on itself. It crumpled and folded, getting smaller and smaller, until in the space of a few seconds it was no bigger than a speck of dust. The speck blinked with one last flash of white light before disappearing completely. The escaping light bathed the cavern, and voices sang from within it.

'The captured life force!' said Gafferty. 'It's been released.'

The three glass bottles, fallen from Mr Ribbons's other hand, crashed to the floor of the arena and shattered. Some of the life force flooded over their remains. More life force bathed Crumpeck as he lay in Lady Strigida's arms. His skin began to soften, and at the same time he began to shrink.

'He's turning into a child … a baby!' cried Strigida in astonishment, as she rocked the newly young Smidgenologist. The last of the life force faded away as baby Crumpeck began to cry.

Claudia appeared, her ghost rising from the shards of her bottle, followed by Hinchsniff and Totherbligh. She grew and grew and began to appear more solid.

'Is she … is she coming back to life?' said Quigg.

As she regained her substance, Claudia sailed out of the crater and into the shop, looking down on the Smidgens with her superior smile. But this time it was also a happy, thankful smile. Totherbligh and Hinchsniff, still as ghostly as ever, floated on either side. She reached out a reassuring hand to Noah, who held it gratefully.

'Did you know that was going to happen?' Gafferty called up to Claudia.

'It was a guess,' the thief said. 'But you made it happen, Gafferty.'

'I'm glad you're rid of those bottles. I mean it. You can go back to living and breathing. And you've got your ghosts back too.'

'The freed life force brought me back. It undid the spell Ribbons used to turn me into a ghost. But Totherbligh and Hinchsniff have decided to retire. For good. They've earned their rest.' The two henchmen grinned as they began to slowly fade.

'Goodbye, Gafferty,' said Claudia. 'It's been very tiresome knowing you. You won't see us again. However, we'll do you one last favour as a token of thanks for your help ...'

With a rush of cold air, the dwindling ghosts swept up all the rubble from the floor of the cavern and carried it up away with them. When they looked up the Smidgens saw the ceiling of the Smidgenmoot was intact and whole and as good as new.

'Could some bright spark explain to me what I just saw?' said Dad, scratching his head. 'What did the Mirror do to that Mr Ribbons?'

'The Mirror needs life force,' said Gafferty. 'Mr Ribbons – whatever he was – he wasn't really alive. Claudia told me that.'

'A creature made of dark magic,' said Lady Strigida, her little finger acting as a dummy for Crumpeck. 'A corrupt and rotten magic.'

'So the Mirror got more than it bargained for when it

tried to steal life force from him,' said Will.

'Yes,' said Gafferty. 'It found itself filling with death magic instead. The more it tried to find life force the more death magic it drew inside. It was too much for it. We couldn't destroy it from the outside, but it could destroy itself from within.'

'It was clever of you to work that out,' said Quigg.

'It was a gamble,' said Gafferty. 'The biggest use of Rule Four I've ever made.'

There would be no sleep for anyone that night. All the Smidgens had come to the Smidgenmoot to meet, talk and, where necessary, shake hands or hug one another. Some had brought food and drink. Some had brought flutes and harps. Songs were being sung, shared and rediscovered. The whole chamber was lit by lamps: light stones and candle stubs shone in crevices in the rock. It was the first time Gafferty had seen the place illuminated by warm, natural light instead of the unearthly magical light of the Mirror. It was no longer a haunted place, a place of bad memory and cursed history. It was a place of harmony and fellowship, as it was originally meant to be.

Mum and Dad had brought Gobkin and Grub, so the whole of the Hive Clan were present along with the Burrow and the Roost. It would have been nice to have Noah there too, although that wasn't really possible. Firstly he was safely tucked up in bed, thanks to the Burrow Smidgens who had been protecting him. And secondly there was no way he could have fit into the space. Nevertheless, it had been decided to make him an honorary Smidgen of all three clans to reward him for his bravery and his friendship.

Lady Strigida stood on the platform at the centre of the chamber. All traces of the stone arch had been removed. The old lady still held baby Crumpeck, who, thankfully, was snoring soundly. She held up her free hand and the music stopped as everyone listened to what she had to say.

'Crumpeck, for all his faults, has been given a second chance,' she began. 'He will get to live his life again from the start, in the heart of our united family. Perhaps he will make mistakes, but at least it will be a life away from the influence of the evil Mirror. That is gone forever.

'And we Smidgens get a second chance too. A chance to work and live together in peace, sharing our knowledge and leaving behind the troubles of the past.

It is all because of one individual, one Smidgen to whom we must give our thanks. Gafferty Sprout!'

Cheers echoed around the cavern as Gafferty stepped on to the platform, watched proudly by her family and friends. The noise lifted her heart, and she knew deep within her that if, in the future, she ever found herself all alone, she would never feel lonely again.

25

A Beginning

A couple of days later Gafferty watched from the top of the chocolate factory as the sun rose over the town. The light slowly cascaded over the rooftops, painting them gold one by one until the whole world was daubed in soft, buttery colours. Its warmth touched her face, and she couldn't help smiling; it felt like the morning was giving her a hug.

Black shapes of birds were slowly circling overhead, their wings lifted by the air currents. One silhouette swooped down towards her and came to rest rather heavily nearby.

'An expert landing as usual,' she said. Will unstrapped himself from the glider and came to sit next to her.

'So you're definitely going then.' He glanced at the bag by her side. She had packed it earlier with everything she needed. It had felt odd not to have the glass knife in there, like there was a piece of her missing, but then she remembered what it had been a part of and was happy to let it go. As a replacement, Dad had given her his own knife, made from the blade of a Big Folk pencil sharpener. It was one of his most valued possessions and Gafferty understood what a precious gift it was. *Look after it and it will look after you*, he had said.

'Yes, I'm going.' She didn't look at Will in case she was ambushed by some annoying tears. There had been a lot of them since the Mirror had been destroyed. 'Do you remember when we first met, all those months ago, and you told me there were other Big Folk towns out there? That there was an entire world beyond this place?'

Will nodded.

'It took you by surprise,' he said. 'I thought everyone knew that.'

'I didn't. It didn't just take me by surprise. It completely shook apart everything I'd ever known. It made me feel so small. Finding the clans helped me feel a part of something bigger. But I still need to see more. I want to see everything, Will. I want to see the whole world. I want to see just how big *big* is. And that's why I'm leaving.'

Will smiled.

'I'm not sure even the whole world is big enough for you, Gafferty. You'll never stop – I expect you'll be the first Smidgen on the moon!'

They both laughed. Then Will said:

'Everyone is going to miss you. Even Quigg will miss you. And you know I will too. I'll miss all our arguing!'

Gafferty laughed again.

'No, you won't! And anyway, you'll be far too busy now that you're a glider trainer. It's hard to believe Lady Strigida gave you that job after all the crashes you've had.'

'I think that's why she gave me the job. Anyone who can crash and live to tell the tale must be doing something right. Wyn's also been made a trainer – we'll be working together. And you'll never guess who my first pupil is: Quigg! She says she wants to see the world from a different angle, so maybe she's taking after you.'

'Watch out, or she'll be putting Norbert in a glider.'

They sat in silence for a while, watching the sun slowly climb higher. Going travelling hadn't been a difficult decision to make, but it had been difficult for Gafferty to tell everyone. Mum and Dad had gone through shock, anger, resignation and understanding in the space of an hour, although Dad had mostly stayed in the anger phase. But he had to admit they didn't need Gafferty to be around as much, at least not for helping out. Some of the Smidgen refugees from the Roost Clan and others from the Burrow had asked if they could come and live in the Hive and start a new life there. The old clan loyalties didn't seem as important any more. Consequently, after many long years, the Hive's sad, empty rooms would be filled with noise and activity once more. The Sprout family would have neighbours, people they could turn to, and Gobkin and Grub would have the playmates she'd never known.

'You've given us a gift,' Mum had said through her tears. 'The gift of a community, and it's only right we should gift you some freedom in return.'

Gobkin was far too busy running around with his new friends to be too interested in Gafferty leaving.

'If I hear of any explosions happening somewhere, I'll know you're probably involved,' was all he said. Grub also seemed unconcerned. Much to Gafferty's horror, he had become firm friends with baby Crumpeck, who had been adopted by a neighbouring family. She dreaded to think what they might be plotting together in their gurgling baby talk.

The first workers at the chocolate factory were starting

to arrive. They looked so small from where the two sat that they could almost be Smidgens.

'Do you know where you're going to go first?' asked Will.

'I'm going to see something called The Sea,' said Gafferty. 'Noah and his family are going to take a trip there and I'm going with them. Noah says he's made a special travelling compartment in his bag for me, complete with a bed. It sounds like I'll be going in style.'

'I like Noah,' said Will. 'It just shows not all Big Folk are ridiculous and cruel.'

'It does. Maybe I'll make some more Big Folk friends. And who knows? Strigida said there were stories of other Smidgens in the Big Outside. Maybe I'll go looking for them too.'

'Look out, Smidgens!' Will shouted. 'Gafferty Sprout is on her way! She'll turn your lives upside down, but you'll be glad she did.'

Gafferty elbowed him in the ribs.

'We're leaving this morning, so I need to get going.' She gave a little sad sniff. 'I just wanted to say goodbye to the town properly and see one last sunrise before I went.'

'Let me give you a lift to Noah's house in the glider,' said Will. 'And I promise that this time we won't crash.'

'Thank you,' said Gafferty. 'I would like that very much.' And she gave him a hug.

As they soared up over the town, Gafferty glanced back at the factory that hid her home. She had spent a couple of hours before sunrise on the roof, finishing a project that had kept her busy for the past few days. She had found an old paint pot amongst some forgotten tools and had used what remained of the paint to write a message, the letters so big they could be seen by anyone who might be passing overhead, whether Smidgen, bird or, perhaps, human. It was a message to the world, a message that said that although the Smidgens might be hidden from the eyes of the Big Folk, they were very much present and a force to be reckoned with:

LITTLE PEOPLE, BIG HEART.

Acknowledgements

I'd like to thank everyone at Bloomsbury Children's Books who has looked after me these last few years, with special thanks to Ellen Holgate, who originally introduced me to the Bloomsbury family. I don't think readers realise just how many people work so hard behind the scenes to turn a writer's idea into a thing of paper that can be bought and borrowed and read. A film always has a long list of credits at its end and I think books should have the same sort of thing, so here goes:

THE SMIDGENS UNITED
A Bloomsbury Children's Books Production

David O'Connell – Writer
Seb Burnett – Illustrator

Lucy Mackay-Sim – Commissioning Editor
Zöe Griffiths – Editorial Director
Jadene Squires – Editorial Assistant

Juliette Rechatin – Designer
Fliss Stevens – Managing Editor
Jessica White – copy-editor
Anna Swan – proofreader
Emily Marples – Senior Publicity Manager
Isi Tucker – Publicity Assistant
Jearl Boatswain – Children's Campaign Assistant
Michael Young – Production Manager

Finally, to all the booksellers, librarians and teachers who
work so hard getting books into children's hands – thank
you! You do a brilliant job.

Have you read

The first book in the hilarious, magical series about tiny people having ENORMOUS adventures!

'A twenty-first century take on *The Borrowers*, albeit much funnier. There is SO much to love about this terrific story … humour and charm, wonderful characterisation and such clever disguises' – Red Reading Hub

Turn the page for a sneak peek …

1

Hunter and Prey

'We'll never do it!' moaned Gobkin. He threw his spear down into the quagmire of dirt, hair and congealed fat surrounding his feet, where it landed with a dull *splot* sound. 'It's *hopeless*.'

Gafferty Sprout counted down from five in her head. She looked at her little brother, his scared face criss-crossed with shadows cast by the grille that covered the extractor pipe in which they were hidden. Warm, greasy light oozed through the metal lattice and dribbled gleaming spots on to the lenses of Gobkin's goggles. Or was that the glistening of his frightened tears?

Be patient with him, Dad had said to her before the two of them had set out on the expedition. *He's young,*

1

but he must learn our ways. Gafferty was learning more about Gobkin's ways, so far. Annoying little snivel-scrap! He'd moaned and whined all the way through the tunnel. He'd griped and groaned as they scaled the wall to get to the pipe. He'd grumbled and groused as they squeezed through the conveniently sized hole cut in its side. He'd carped and bellyached as they passed the now useless fan that Dad had carefully detached on a previous visit. It was Gobkin's first time properly out in the Big World and he was acting like it was bath night!

Dad had taken Gafferty out on her first hunt. She'd been brave. The oldest child had to be brave. If something happened to Mum or Dad, then she would be the one in charge. Gobkin was different. He was three years younger than Gafferty, and Mum and Dad had spoilt him, protected him. But that had all changed six months ago, when their little brother, Grub, had been born. A creature of snot and bad temper, he now took up all their parents' time. Gobkin was no longer the youngest. Gobkin needed to grow up.

Gafferty sighed irritably. This would be a lot easier if he weren't so much younger than her. But then, she had never known anyone of her own age. It was a constant annoyance, not having anyone who understood what she was feeling. Almost as much of a constant annoyance as Gobkin. Her hands toyed anxiously with the strap of her scavenger bag. The truth was that she was feeling nervous, and having a miserable, insecure assistant with her made it worse.

'I've done this a hundred times, you fimbling grizzle-head!' she said finally, summoning the effort to sound confident. 'Well, once or twice. Even three or four times. Lots of times. Maybe.'

'And Dad was with you then.'

'Don't worry, Gob. It'll be easy. I know what I'm doing.' She peered through the grille at the activity taking place in the noisy kitchen on its other side. 'And I have our prey in my sights.'

Gobkin leaned forward, his curiosity getting the better of him.

'Where … ?' he began.

Without warning, a shadow fell over the grille.

'Humans!' hissed Gafferty. She threw her arms protectively around her brother and dragged him backwards through the muck. They crouched in the darkness, frozen with fear, trying not to breathe in the rancid stench of their surroundings.

A gigantic eye stared through the grille. Gobkin

squealed and even Gafferty gave a sharp intake of breath. The eye frowned, blinked, then disappeared. Before the children had time to act, an enormous finger, wider and taller than either of them, rammed against the grille, sending a rattling echo down the pipe. Gafferty and Gobkin covered their ears as the finger hit the metal mesh once more.

'Oi, Barry!' boomed a voice. 'Is this extractor broken again?'

'Aye, boss,' called Barry, from somewhere in the kitchen. 'Keeps getting fixed, keeps getting broken. Mice, I reckon.'

'Mice?' snapped the boss. 'Got screwdrivers, have they? Don't let anyone hear you talk about mice, or we'll be closed down.' The voice grew quieter. The giant was moving away from the pipe. 'And where would we be without McGreasy's Burgers? Where would everyone go for their chips then, eh?'

'I don't think I'll ever get used to Big Folk,' whispered Gobkin, getting to his feet and reaching for his spear, 'with their great big stomping feet and humongous bottoms wobbling about overhead. And always shouting about everything! Why can't everyone be like us? Smidgens. Too small to cause any trouble ...'

4

'But big enough to care.' Gafferty finished their dad's often-repeated adage. She saw Gobkin's eyes shine as his brain caught up.

'Chips,' he said. 'They're making *chips*.'

'Chips,' confirmed Gafferty, nodding. 'Our prey. Golden, plump and crispy, completely defenceless, and ours for the taking. That's what we're hunting today. One chip will do nicely for dinner for all of us.'

'And don't forget the *kurrisorce*,' said Gobkin, drooling slightly. 'I read about it in *The Big Book of Big Folk Facts*. Humans love *kurrisorce*. The book says it channels the power of the mythical Kurri, god of chips.'

Gafferty smiled. That was more like it. Gobkin always had his nose in a book. Sometimes he talked like one. And now that he had survived a risky encounter with the Big Folk, his hunger was making him bolder. They pressed their faces against the grille and stared out at the Big World.

Rule One of the Smidgens: *stay hidden and observe*. From inside the extractor fan they could watch the goings-on of the burger bar. There were two chefs – Barry and his boss – cooking the burgers and sausages on the griddle, and frying chips, nuggets and anything else anyone cared to batter and fry in a deep vat of boiling oil.

5

Dealing with humans – who were at least twenty times as tall as you – was a dangerous business for all manner of reasons. If you weren't dodging human feet, then there were human-made death-traps. You could easily end up as a Smidgen-fritter if you weren't careful.

A counter separated the kitchen from the shop, where customers waited for their orders. Gafferty had chosen a quiet time for the hunt when the cooks were preparing food in readiness for the evening rush. There were no customers, and that meant fewer eyes to see them.

'It's time,' she said. 'Let the hunt begin.'

2

Into the Frying Pan

Rule Two of the Smidgens: *don't do anything flipping stupid.* That was easier said than done.

'Get the rope out,' Gafferty said, taking command. Whilst Gobkin rummaged obediently in his pack for a coil of stolen fishing line, she made last-minute adjustments to her scavenger suit.

Pulling on a couple of laces on either side of her waistcoat, she drew out four tubes of material from hidden pockets so that they dangled freely about her, making it look like she had grown extra arms. Then she drew her hood over her short red hair, a hood spotted with velvet eyes. Her clothes were a soft grey colour, like that of the spider she was meant to resemble. Admittedly,

7

she was quite big for a spider, just as Gobkin was quite big to be the fly that formed his disguise, with his goggles and wing-shaped backpack and furry leggings, but the Smidgens never intended for themselves to be seen at all. *It's in case someone catches a glimpse of you from the corner of their eye,* as Mum said. *If the Big Folk see a shape that they think they recognise, they won't bother looking too closely.*

All Sprout family members picked their creepy-crawly guise at a young age and, once decided, stayed loyal to it. Dad was a beetle, Mum was a ladybird and Grub was – appropriately, given the amount of slime he produced – a slug. At least for now. Gobkin had toyed with being a grasshopper for a while, but had decided on a housefly, for their speed and dexterity. And he said they had a fascinating way of digesting their food, which had sounded disgusting to Gafferty when Gob had described it to them in detail at the dinner table.

With her bag slung round her shoulder, Gafferty was finally ready. Gobkin handed her the rope.

'Let's get this over with,' he said, biting his lip.

Gafferty flicked the catch on the grille (another bit of Dad's handiwork, along with the hinges that turned the metal grid into a door) and carefully pulled it open. The two cooks were busy at the griddle, their backs turned to the chip fryer. The coast was clear. Gafferty secured one end of the rope around a rivet poking up from the floor of the pipe. She let the remainder drop into the heavy, oily air of the kitchen.

It was a short but nervous climb down from the extractor fan. They touched ground on a box of plastic gloves that sat on a shelf beneath the pipe, along with supplies of sauce, mayonnaise and mustard. As they paused for breath behind a ketchup bottle, Gafferty said: 'Mum uses those gloves to make waterproof clothing. I could stuff one into my bag on the way back, but I don't want to make things too complicated. We're here for the chips. Carrying too much will slow us down.'

Gobkin nodded.

'Rule Three of the Smidgens: *be ready to run, and run fast,*' he recited.

They scurried along the shelf to its end. Then it was just a

quick jump into a soft pile of paper napkins that were heaped on the kitchen counter below, followed by a short dash across the counter to the deep fat fryer, its oil boiling with the menace of a restive volcano. They'd almost made it!

A bell chimed through the shop. Gobkin looked at his sister in alarm.

'The door!' hissed Gafferty. 'There's a customer! That's all we need.'

They dived into the shadow of a large salt shaker sitting next to the fryer. Gafferty peeped around its curved edge. It was a boy, barely visible behind the glass countertop, its surface misted with steam. One of the human cooks lumbered over from the griddle. It was Barry, judging from his voice.

'And what can I do for you, young lad?' he said, leaning over the counter to greet the customer.

'Small portion of chips, please,' said the boy, too busy picking his nose to pay attention to anything else.

'Coming up,' said Barry in reply. 'You're in luck – there's a batch just about ready.'

He turned to the fryer, his shadow plunging Gafferty and Gobkin's hiding place into darkness. They cowered behind the salt shaker, Gafferty's heart thumping like a drum in her chest. Next to her, Gobkin gripped his spear tightly to stop himself from shaking with terror. She put her hand on his shoulder to reassure him – he mustn't lose his nerve now! But what could they do? The human was bound to see them if they stayed here!

Barry took a sheet of greaseproof paper and laid it on the counter next to the salt shaker. The edges of the paper curled upwards. It gave Gafferty an idea, a risky one, but it might save them. Rule Four of the Smidgens: *if in doubt, make it up!*

The cook lifted the metal basket of chips from the fryer, shaking it to drain the excess oil. Using a large scoop, he shovelled a portion on to the paper. Globules of hot fat spat from the golden pile of fried potato, one fizzing dangerously close to Gobkin's ear.

'I want to go home!' he squeaked.

Gafferty grabbed his arm. She knew what was about to happen next.

'Get ready to run,' she whispered.

As she expected, Barry turned to the chip buyer.

'Would you like them salted?' he said.

Gafferty didn't wait to listen for the reply.

'Now!' she hissed. She dragged Gobkin away from the salt shaker and dived beneath the curl of the chip paper.

11

They crawled on their bellies under its cover, sweating in the heat radiating from the freshly cooked food sitting on its surface. Gobkin had just pulled his foot out of view when Barry turned back and reached for the shaker that had been their hiding place moments before. Salt hailed over the chips, rattling on to the paper above their heads. Her elbows hurting with effort, Gafferty wriggled across to the far side where the chip wrapper brushed up against a huge tub of margarine. Again, she waited for the moment when she knew Barry's back would be turned.

'And vinegar?' she heard him ask the hungry customer. That was it! She jumped up and scrambled behind the tub, pulling Gobkin along with her. The two of them sank to their knees, panting for breath.

Vinegar showered over the chips nearby. Gafferty grabbed the spear that Gobkin still clutched tightly. She'd not forgotten why they were there. Barry was now folding up the paper into a neat package, spinning it around as he tucked in the corners. He'd had so much practice he could make the creases in the wrapper without looking, something that Gafferty planned to use to her advantage. As the half-finished parcel of food turned towards them, she stabbed the nearest chip with lightning speed, a spider ambushing its victim, and hauled it free. Gobkin, who had watched with amazement, helped her drag it into their hiding place.

'And that,' said Gafferty, grinning as her brother eyed their still-warm, golden prize, 'is what I call a takeaway.'

And don't miss

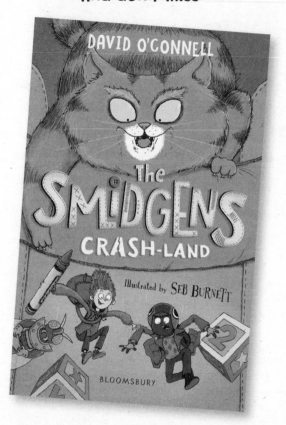

Crash-land with the Smidgens in the second book in David O'Connell's funny and magical series about tiny people having ENORMOUS adventures!

OUT NOW!

Have you read all
THE DUNDOODLE
MYSTERIES?

AVAILABLE NOW